WALKOUT

CAROLINE SPRINGS CHARTER

LILA ROSE

CHAPTER ONE

DALLAS

*W*hy in the fuck did I get on the plane to chase some pussy? I had no clue, except when I saw Melissa snarling something at her motherfucking *husband* in the restaurant, I realised I wanted that for me. Her attitude. Her fucking tiny, stunning body, her shoulder-length hair where I could wrap my fist in it while I claimed her mouth. Just like I wanted to claim her body and mind.

How-fucking-ever, she was strong-minded enough to not be claimed anywhere but maybe the bedroom. I'd have to see if she'd heel for me behind closed doors.

The matter of her being married was an obstacle I could push over. Still, it was a pain in the fucking arse.

She hadn't worn her ring when she was back in Melbourne helping us find Nary, Vicious's woman, because I would have noticed something like that. So why had she hidden it? And why in the hell had she acted the way she did with me, like she wanted me inside her, when she was already taken?

None of it made sense, but I was going to get to the bottom of it.

Melissa was mine.

She'd decided to run when I told her not to. I'd fucking told her I'd claimed her as my woman. She had to have known I'd follow and find out she was playing some sort of game.

A game I was determined to win.

"Fuck," I clipped, and ran a hand over my face before picking up my whisky neat and taking a sip. Who would have thought I'd be chasing pussy? Not me in a goddamn million years. Yet, there I was. As soon as she turned up in Melbourne and gave me her attitude, I knew she was it. Even if I denied it so many fucking times, she'd gotten under my skin and once she was there, I couldn't stop thinking about her.

So whatever the shit was with her being married, I'd get it sorted and take her home with me.

A chair on each side of me pulled out. Glancing to Knife and then Beast, I lifted my chin and said, "Good to have you here, brothers."

Beast gave me a chin lift back. He never said a word. However, he had no trouble communicating what he wanted in his actions or texts.

"Glad to help out, brother," Knife answered. "What's the plan?"

Dodge, President of the Hawks MC Caroline Springs Charter, had sent Beast and Knife to Sydney as soon as I'd called him asking for some backup. It was good to have a family who would drop anything to do whatever you asked.

I had that in the army. Trevor Boon was a brother, but he didn't stick around once we'd helped Beth Cliff out of her shit in Ballarat with Stoke and Mally. Still, I understood Trevor had his own family shit to deal with, which was why I'd stuck with the Hawks back then. I wanted somewhere to belong, and I'd found it within the Hawks MC. I liked what I saw, the connection and safety they brought one another. So I stayed, until I moved to Melbourne to help Dodge out with his shit. There'd been a few scum-suckers we had to clean out of the brotherhood, but now it was living free. I stayed in Melbourne. Guessed it was the best decision since I got to meet my tiny woman in the end.

Though, I'd soon see if chasing her was going to be the right move.

If whatever the shit she was playing was going to bring trouble breathing down the Hawks' neck, I'd cut her loose.

"We're staking out Melissa's place tonight. Want in there with you two at my back. I have to find out why she has a wedding ring on her fuckin' finger when she didn't wear one back in Melbourne."

"Done." Knife nodded and gestured to a waiter ordering him and Beast a beer. Once he'd done it, he slouched in his seat and asked, "She know you're here yet?"

I snorted. "Nope."

Knife smiled. "How'd you see her ring then?"

"I may be a big motherfucker, but I can be smoke when I want to be. Caught a glimpse when I followed her into the drug store the other day."

"This shit is weird. Anyone with eyes could tell she had a thing for you back in Melbourne."

Beast nodded in agreement.

"I guess we'll have answers one way or another tonight," I bit out as I watched my tiny woman hiss something else at her husband and storm out. I didn't miss the tears shining in her eyes either, no matter how far away I was. At the door, she paused.

Fuck, had she made us?

"Clear," I barked low.

My brothers moved in different directions while I slid out of my seat and under the fucking table. I wasn't ready for her to see me, not until I had answers. So if that meant I had to make a fool out of myself by hiding in shit places, then I would.

There was a story behind Melissa's deceit, and I couldn't wait to find out about it.

When I saw the coast was clear, I sat back up and finished my drink. Knife and Beast appeared with fresh drinks, and Beast slid a spare one my way while Knife talked on his phone.

"He's here. We don't know anything yet. Okay." He sighed. "It's Julian."

Tipping my head back, I closed my eyes to the ceiling and cursed under my breath. I did not want to have to deal with Julian, but I knew if I fuckin' didn't, he'd be on the phone to his girl, *my* woman, and she'd find out I was in town too early.

Taking the phone, I glared at Knife's smile and answered, "Yo?"

"What in the flaming hell is going on? You're in Sydney chasing my bestie and I hear she's married? As in *married*, married, with a ring on her finger and all? How could she not tell me? Do you need me to come there and slap some sense into her? I will. I'm ready to do some shaking and hair pulling to figure out what in the Jesus Christ is going on in her sweet little brain."

"Who told you?"

"Dallas." He sighed out my name; it sounded like he thought I was stupid. "You listen to me and listen well. I'm a part of the pussy posse. Nothing, and I mean *nothing*, doesn't find its way to my ears. I hear all when I have my girls at my back. Doesn't matter who told me, they're all protected by their hot males in their beds. What matters is if you need me to come take the wench out? What was she thinking? Why would she get married and not tell me shit? I mean really, what the fuck is up with that?"

"Stand down, Julian. If I can't work out what's going on, I'll call you in. But for now, know I *will* get to the bottom of this, and she'll be with me back in Melbourne soon."

"Good," he snapped. "I swear when she was here all I heard about was you. So to learn she's married does not jive well. Something is happening, and it's big. Take care with her, hero man, or you'll be dealing with me ringing you every day for the rest of your life."

Cringing at the thought, I then snorted and reminded him, "You were talking about knocking some sense into her not that long ago."

"That's different. You want to drag her back to your lair, bang her and claim her. All I want is to be her BFF for life. You'll be the one with her all the time, not me. You need to treat her with care if you want to keep in her panties. Hear me?"

"Fuckin' hell. Yeah, I get you and that kinda shits me."

"Aw, it's okay. Now you're going to be *doing* my BFF, you'll *get me* a lot more since I'll be travelling your way to see her."

"Do you want me to continue my play for Melissa or run for the fuckin' hills?"

"Play."

"Then do not threaten me."

"How is my time a threat?" he huffed.

"Forget it. I gotta get shit done, Julian."

"Okey dokey. Once you do, tell her I'm way pissed."

With a sigh, I closed my eyes and rubbed at my temple. "Done," I said before hanging up.

The first thing I saw was Beast's shoulders shaking and knew he was silently laughing, while Knife threw his head back and just roared with it a few beats after I'd hung up.

"You wanna get a flight back now and leave her be?"

5

Clenching my jaw, I snapped my glare to Knife.

He whistled low. "Damn, she must'a got under your skin if you're willing to put up with Julian as her close friend."

I narrowed my eyes even more, but he just burst out laughing.

Flicking my gaze to Beast, I saw he was sitting there smiling.

Sighing aloud, I scrubbed a hand over my face. "What in the fuck am I thinkin'?"

Knife snorted. "Hoping she'll be your sunshine like the rest of the brothers have found."

"Maybe it'd be better to keep on as is," I said more to myself than my brothers. Then I thought of Melissa and how she'd sunk her claws in with her sass and smartarse mouth. She was embedded deep, and I couldn't seem to unhinge those fucking claws.

If her reason for why she lied wasn't good enough, I'd walk away and wash her from my mind.

If the reason for the lie was one I understood and could stand by, I'd get her out, make her safe, and make her mine.

She wanted me. I wanted her.

It was time to make it happen.

Or at least see if it could happen.

"Nah, man. She's the one. You wouldn't do the chasing like you have otherwise," Knife said, and I saw Beast nod.

Rubbing a hand over my face, I said, "Let's head to the hotel. We'll get you two a room and then stake out her and his place. I'll go in if they're not there. If they are, we'll wait until they're asleep. Beast has my back in the house. Knife, need you on lookout. See anything fishy, text, and we'll get out."

Knife nodded. "Sounds like a plan."

Standing, I smirked and said, "By the way, the hotel we're stayin' at has some convention thing happenin'. You two have'ta share a room."

"What the fuck, brother?" Knife glared.

"Soon as Dodge said he was sending you two, I went and asked about a room. They had one left and it's a double bed one."

Knife groaned as he stood next to me. "Have you not seen our brother here? He's fucking huge, and you expect me to share a bed with the big motherfucker?"

"Well, I ain't sharin' mine." I laughed.

"Cold, brother. We're here to help, and you deal us this crap. If I'm looking thin in the morning, you'll know why. Beast would have squished me in my sleep."

Shoving him in the shoulder, I told him, "Stop being a pussy. Not like Beast here is complaining." My phone chimed.

Beast: I'll go stay at another hotel.

Shaking my head, I said, "No. Need you close."

He stood and pumped out another text. **I'll find one close by.**

Knife, looking over my shoulder, said, "Don't worry about it, brother. We'll go top and tail."

Beast glared and typed something else as we headed out the restaurant. **I ain't fucking smelling your feet, arsehole.**

Throwing my head back, I laughed. Fuck, it was good to have my brothers there. It helped ease some of my stress.

CHAPTER TWO

DALLAS

*I*t was a little after midnight when we made our way to my tiny woman's place. My mind refused to truly register she had a goddamn ring on her finger, not until I knew why she hadn't been wearing it back in Melbourne.

I sent a chin lift to Knife towards the road, and then another to Beast, and he shifted off to around the back of the large ranch style house in the middle of the bloody city. From my time in the army and on a special-forces team not many knew about, I'd learned many skills. One being I was able to move around undetected, despite my bulk.

To start with, I checked all the front windows. I clenched my jaw, pissed when I found all were shut and locked tight. Without another way in, I risked the front door. Getting to my knees, I slid the tools out of my back pocket and just as I was about to get to work, the door flew open. A pair of biker boots was the first thing I saw. Glancing up, Beast was looking down at me, smirking with a raised brow.

The fucker managed to get in before me.

Rolling my eyes, I stood. Beast shifted to the side and closed the door behind me. His hand came down on my shoulder before I moved off. Meeting his gaze, he touched his ear and then threw his hands out like a bomb going off.

"Alarm?" I mouthed.

He nodded, then sliced his finger across his neck. It told me he'd already disabled it. Hell, maybe our brother could walk through fucking walls and cut any alarm down with one look while I twiddled my thumbs checking the windows out front.

It was likely.

Jutting my chin up and out, he disappeared down to the right of the house, while I took the left. My first room was the living room. I looked around and noticed a lack of photos. Not even a wedding photo was displayed. The place was neat and tidy, sterile in fact. Did they even live in the house? Obviously I knew they did because I'd staked them out enough to know where they worked, ate, and resided.

For the past week, they'd come back to this house each night, yet the place didn't look lived in. It was as if they only existed there.

Creeping out of the living area, I went into the kitchen. The same vibe was present, a room that felt cold.

The house wasn't a home.

I shook my head. Nothing was adding up.

Down the hall, I went to the last room knowing it would be the main bedroom. Placing my ear against the door, I listened and heard nothing but a soft snore behind it. Christ, I didn't want to go in and see my woman in bed with another man, but I had to.

Fuck, if she was curled up happily next to him, I'd leave her to it, despite wanting answers to why she'd played the flirt with me.

If she looked content in bed with another man, it meant she wasn't for me. Which, for some fucked reason, sent a pang through my chest.

Slowly and quietly, I opened the door just an inch. All I saw was a door to either the robe or bathroom and some chest drawers. Listening, I caught another snuffle of a snore, so knowing I hadn't woken anyone, I opened it further and stuck my head in. The bed was over by the huge-arse windows. The open blinds helped me make out the shape in bed.

There was only one.

Their back was to me, and the covers were pulled all the way up. Her dickwad was on the smaller-size build, so I didn't know if it was Melissa or him. Though, if it was only one of them, where in the hell was the other?

With every step I took closer to the bed, my pulse raced harder; adrenaline was riding my arse.

At the side of the bed, my lungs seized. It wasn't her.

Then where in the fuck was she?

Glaring down at the fucker in the bed, I wondered yet again what he had on her. It had to be something for her to lie about being married. Shit, she hadn't even told Julian about him. She probably didn't want to worry a single soul about what was happening in her life.

Too bad she never thought I'd actually follow up on my threat and follow her.

Heading back to the door, I was just out the room and closing the door behind me when I sensed someone coming my way. Before I took to hiding, I glanced around and saw Beast strolling down the hall. From the light of the moon shining in the many damn windows around the house, I could see my brother was pissed about something.

He jerked his head towards the way he'd just come. I followed without a sound back down the hall, past the kitchen and down another hall to the room at the other end of the long house.

The door was open, meaning Beast had already been in there. Otherwise, like all the other rooms off the halls, the door would have been closed.

Before I went to enter, Beast's hand came down on my shoulder. He turned me to face him and his other hand landed on my other shoulder. His hard eyes met mine and he gave me a gentle shake, keeping my stare.

Fuck me.

Whatever was in that room was going to piss me off.

He wanted me to have my head.

Nodding, I started to move, until he shook his head and gave me a chin lift. With my own hard glare, I nodded again and took a deep breath.

His hands dropped, and I moved in. Beast wasn't far behind me. I felt his heat.

Fucking hell.

His action told me what I was about to see wouldn't only just piss me off, but it'd set me off to want to kill a person.

Fisting and releasing my hands, I stretched my neck and stepped further into the room. It was similar to the main bedroom, only it was the opposite. The bed was to the left under the big windows. A small figure was curled up into a ball on the bed with no covers over them.

Melissa.

She had on sleep pants and a long-sleeved tee. As I got closer, I sucked back a sharp breath and felt Beast's hand on my back.

Her face was marred with bruises.

Bruises she hadn't had at the restaurant.

They were new.

Fuck me.

They were new.

I could have stopped it from happening and taken her with me when I'd had the chance.

Christ, I had a lot of chances in the past week to nab her and take her home with me. Seeing her with black, purple, and brown bruises on her face stabbed me deep in the chest because I knew, I fuckin' knew, I could have stopped it from happening.

Jesus.

I got to my knees on the side of the bed, and with the light outside her room from the street lamp, I could see she'd cried herself to sleep. Her cheeks were still wet. She hadn't long drifted off and was no doubt in pain because even in her sleep she wore a frown.

My head dropped, my chin touching my chest. I sucked in another breath.

My woman was sleeping in pain while the fucker down the other end slept like he didn't have a care in the world.

That was going to change.

He'd care.

He'd definitely care because I'd make sure he did.

And if he still didn't in the end, then he'd breathe no longer.

A hand came down on the back of my neck. Glancing up and around, Beast rose his brow. He wanted to know how we were going to deal with it.

I didn't have a fuckin' clue.

Melissa was smart. If she could have, she would have gotten out of an abusive relationship. Fuck, she'd even kick the shit out of the person who'd try crap with her. So there was something I was missing. Something that was keeping her where she was.

I had to find out what it was.

Only, how did I go about doing it?

Did I take her from this fucked up place and risk whatever was holding her there?

No. Before anything, I needed to get my answers right from the source.

Tensing, I watched her shift slightly on the bed and then wince from it. I took out my phone and texted Knife: **Found her beaten in a room. Need to find out what the fuck is going on. Need a closer eye on the place, all the way around. Be fast and silent.**

Knife: **Will do, brother. You taking her out tonight?**

Me: **No. Something's keeping her here. Gotta find out what and now.**

Knife: **Go gentle.**

Shaking my head, I glared down at my phone and typed back: **She's mine. I know how to treat her.**

At least I hoped.

Being around women for long periods of time wasn't something I liked or wanted.

Until her.

Beast's hand came into view, he was asking for the phone. I handed it over and watched him read it. He gave me his eyes after and nodded. He was down with the play.

There was no way I could walk out of that room to leave my tiny woman with that fucker. Not after seeing her like that. Not until she knew I was there and if need be, I'd have her back.

Glancing to Beast, I jerked my chin towards the door. He nodded and made his way out of the room, shutting the door behind him. He'd keep an eye on the inside while Knife took the outside. That left me with a small amount of time to wake my woman and find out what in the fuck was going down.

Fear reared its ugly head inside me. Fear that she'd wake and tell me to get the fuck out. That she liked where she was, and the way she had been with me was just her messing about.

Rolling back my shoulders, I shook out the tension.

What I was about to do would get my arse kicked from her,

13

and I looked forward to it because I hated the thought of scaring her after what had just been done to her.

"Tiny," I whispered into the room. Her brows furrowed down. Gently, steering clear of her bruises, I ran my finger from the top of her hairline in the middle of her forehead to down between her eyes and then to the tip of her nose. Her posture relaxed, something I wasn't going for, but it was also something I liked a fucking lot because it meant she felt soothed from my touch. I tried again. Resting my chin on the bed, I whispered, "Tiny woman."

Her eyes fluttered, and then she shifted back fast, her mouth opened wide as if to scream. I moved just as quickly and got on the bed over her, with my hand covering her mouth.

"It's me. Calm the fuck down. It's me."

Shit, I hoped she knew.

She blinked a few more times, looking up at me. Her eyes cleared and became confused. Slowly, I removed my hand from her mouth.

"Tiny, I have a few questions you need to answer."

Her head tilted to its side on the bed. I shifted back, sitting my arse on the mattress while she got to her elbows.

"Viking man?"

"Yeah, woman." I smiled, only it faded quickly when she sat, winced, and then threw her fist towards my face. It would have collided with my nose if I hadn't grabbed it. "The fuck?" I clipped low.

"What are you doing here in the middle of the night and scaring the crap out of me? You're going to ruin everything."

"I told you I'd claimed you and was coming after you. Ain't my fuckin' fault you didn't listen."

Her eyes widened and she winced again. Her free hand reached up and touched her face. Her shoulders sagged, and she ripped her hand free of mine and turned her face away. "You shouldn't have come."

"Bull-fuckin'-shit. Tell me what in the hell is going on." Her head whipped around to face me with a fierce glare. I went on, "If you tell me you love the fucker who put that ring on your finger and did that shit to your face, I'll leave. You tell me this is what you want, and I'll walk out that door never to see you again." When she didn't say anything, I bit out, "Tell me."

It was then her face crumpled and she buried it in her hands as she burst into tears.

Fuck me.

I didn't know what to do with a crying woman.

It made me feel awkward.

But shit, she was the only woman I wouldn't leave to cry it out alone.

And that right there said a lot. Because seeing her break like that, it did shit to me on the inside, and I couldn't handle seeing her tears, hearing her gasping for breath as she sobbed. It fucking hurt me to see it.

Sliding my hand under her arse and the other at her back, I picked her up and placed her in my lap. There I cupped the side of her face and led her to rest her head against my chest.

Hell, fuck the tears. Fuck the woman's emotions. Fuck it all.

I'd put up with it because it was my tiny woman doing it all in my arms.

So when she wrapped her arms around my waist, I knew I was doing an okay job at comforting her. I also knew she wasn't getting rid of me.

CHAPTER THREE

MELISSA

*H*e'd come.

My Viking man had come to claim me as his. I hadn't believed him at the time because every man in my life had either been a prick or up and left without looking back or giving me a reason.

Forgetting me.

Even Julian had forgotten for a while. Of course I understood it, but it didn't mean it hurt less.

Yet, there was one who'd picked me.

Who'd come for *me.*

Followed *me.*

Wanted me.

It was the man cradling me to him while I tried to get myself under control. He held me even though I knew, from his stiff posture, he wasn't comfortable being around a woman who showed their emotions.

He was there and doing something he hated for me.

I couldn't have been happier. Even though my face hurt like a bitch, I was content because I was in Dallas's arms. I'd lost count of the times my thoughts had strayed to him. Wondering what he was doing, who he was doing it with, and where he was.

At first, I thought I had been dreaming his voice. The caress of it across my skin had relaxed me. I'd kept my eyes closed and prayed to hear it again, and when I did, a shiver had tingled over my body.

Seeing and feeling him helped me deal with what was happening. He gave me hope to stay strong for me and Della.

Then again, with hope, there was also dread for Dallas being there. It meant he could get caught up in everything, and I didn't want him to.

It was my problem, and Dallas would be dragged down from being around me. Jimmy would haul Dallas down because of me, and I couldn't let another person be touched in any way by Jimmy.

"Tiny, we don't have much time. I have to get out of here before that fucker wakes for any reason, and I need to know if I'm taking you with me or not?"

Sniffing, I lifted my sleeve and wiped at my nose. "Why would you ask?" I was surprised he was giving me a choice. Then again, he didn't know I would pay anything to be out of the situation I was in if it meant Della and I would stay safe.

He grunted. "I know you don't want to stay. Fuck, your bruises and tears are enough to tell me. So if you'd said no, I'd lug you outta here by your hair if I had to. This situation is poisonous. However, I know something else is at play here. I know you wouldn't stay if you didn't have a good reason."

Shit.

He knew me.

But how?

How did he know I stayed because I had no choice? If I was to save Della, I had to stay and do as I was told.

Della, who had been doing her own undercover work at one of Jimmy's strip clubs had contacted me through a mutual acquaintance because she wasn't getting what she needed. She sought out my services of digging up all the information I could find on Jimmy Vanclove.

Modella Kent, or Della for short, wanted dirt on Jimmy so she could send him away for a long time. She believed he was the one who'd killed her sister.

At first, I was doing it for a job and for the money. It wasn't until I found things out about Jimmy that I made it my own personal mission to put the sick dick away.

Jimmy was well known in Sydney. He owned many businesses in the city, which in turn, told me he owned many people as well. I didn't know how deep it went until the detective I went to handed me right on over to Jimmy.

Jimmy had been watching me watch him.

He liked what I could do with a computer. He liked I could get into places without being noticed.

He also knew it had been my friend Della who had contacted me in the first place because her little sister had gone missing. In the end, when the police had come up with nothing, she'd decided it was up to her to find the truth, which was how she'd become one of his strippers.

Somehow Della's sister had caught Jimmy's attention.

Jimmy liked little girls. Ashley, Della's sister, was a beautiful, sweet girl and only fifteen when she went missing. She was fifteen when he took her from the shopping centre and raped her. She was fifteen when he kept her with him for over six months, using and abusing her.

She was only fifteen when he killed her.

Drowned her.

He made it look like an accident. But I knew, from the footage I found on Jimmy's own personal computer, what had happened.

It was that footage, along with two more I'd found, that I took to the detective over two months ago. I'd been stupid to think Jimmy's hands didn't reach that far. The detective had asked me to take a drive with him. He'd wanted to show me some cases he had, and I'd foolishly followed without another thought. We'd stopped at the house I currently lived in, and when the front door opened with Jimmy standing in it with a smile on his face, I'd tried to make a run for it. I didn't get far. Jimmy had too many men working for him.

As soon as I was in the house and sitting in the living room, Jimmy offered me a job. After I had finished laughing in his face, he smiled a knowing smile, and at the time I didn't know why. I didn't know until he'd explained they had Della and if I didn't work for him, doing anything he wished, she would end up dead, and it would be all my fault. Then if I did choose to be smart, he would leave her alone, only have her doing what she was paid for, working at his strip joint.

I had to protect Della in any way I could, at least until I had more on Jimmy. He'd already destroyed everything I had, including my laptop.

So I picked door number two. I worked in his computer company doing illegal shit for him by finding out everything I could on businesses he wanted to take over.

At first, I had my own place and his men followed me everywhere. Until I had tried to run, to grab Della, and get away from him. It didn't work. Which was how I had become married to Jimmy. He wanted me living under his roof and under his thumb even more.

I was valuable to him.

When he showed me a video of a man beating and raping

Della, I had no choice but to follow through with what he wanted. So I said those vows as he slid his ring on my finger, since he once again promised me Della would stay safe if I did everything he wanted. And if I ran again, it wouldn't be Della receiving the fists or being raped. She'd be dead, and it would be me being used by his men.

However, when Julian rang and I heard his fear, I'd had to do something. It was Julian.

He'd needed my help, and he was one person I would risk my own life for.

Still, I played it smart and went to Jimmy asking him for some time away. Stating that if I didn't help Julian, he would know something was up and he'd come looking for me, which wouldn't be good for Jimmy. I promised to be back in a certain amount of time. At first, I was shocked when he said I could go. But he was smart because he knew I'd come back for Della.

The weeks I'd been away were the best I'd had in a long time.

The best.

Meeting Dallas, my Viking man, and teasing him taught me, no matter who I had to go back to, I was still myself on the inside. The thought to tell not only the Hawks men, but also Mason about what I was dealing with had crossed my mind. Bit it had quickly fled. It was my mess to clean up and I didn't want trouble to be dropped on either clubs. God, they had their own crap to deal with. I wasn't going to add to it.

So I'd enjoyed my time. I'd smiled, had fun, and instantly fell in like with a certain someone.

When I got back, a day late, Jimmy wanted me to learn my lesson for having him worry. He gave me to one of his men, Tate. I was lucky enough that Tate was the only man I could stand. He wasn't bad like the others. So when he took me into my room, he asked me to pretend. I did because the fear of my lack of acting weighed down on me, and if I didn't pull it off, I knew worse would come. I also knew Tate would be allowed to live.

It was only the previous night that I felt the pain of his fists for the first time. We'd been out to dinner and Jimmy had taken a liking to a girl who looked about sixteen. When I refused to steer her away from her family so he could take her, and after I gave him some not so pleasant words in return, he beat me for disobeying him and for also making a scene in front of people.

I didn't care.

I'd take all the pain in the world if it meant I could save a young girl from Jimmy.

"Tiny," Dallas whispered into the room, causing my body to shiver. "Tell me."

Sighing, I gripped his tee to me and I told him. Well, at least the CliffsNotes of what had happened, about the mess I was in along with Della. I told him because I didn't want him to leave and think I'd picked that life for me willingly. I told him because I was scared.

I'd tried to get a way out, a way to find leverage over Jimmy. It took time and I was still looking, only coming up with a small amount of crimes, but nothing solid.

So I told him it all because I cared what he thought of me. He was the first man in many years I wanted in my life, but couldn't keep.

"Now do you see why I can't leave? Not until I know Della is safe. Not until I can find someone who isn't under his thumb in the police force and take him down for all the crimes he's committed. I have to stay and slowly work my way through the fog to end him."

Throughout my explanation I felt Dallas tense, his arms tightened around me, and if I moved, I was certain they would shatter from the force he was keeping them so stiff.

Suddenly the door came open. I gasped and tried to jump

from the bed to take on whoever was coming through so Dallas could run. But his arms held me to him, and when I saw Beast, a member of the Hawks MC, my rapidly beating heart started to slow.

Beast communicated something to Dallas, which caused Dallas to stand and place me next to him on the floor.

"Someone's coming, we need to leave."

"I can't," I whispered urgently.

His jaw clenched, his eyes closed tightly for a second and when he opened them, his gaze was hard. "I know. But I'm not fuckin' leaving, Tiny. I'll do what I can to get you and that woman out and away from him."

"No, you have to leave. He—"

"Enough!" he clipped low and harsh; it hurt to hear him say it like that, but I knew he used that tone because he cared about me. He drew me against him and softened his tone when he said, "I'm here, you're mine. No one fucks with what's mine. I plan to take the motherfucker down, and I'll do it smiling knowing what he did to you."

I worried my bottom lip with my teeth and noticed Beast at my window doing something to it before it slid open without the alarm going off.

Shifting back, I glanced up to Dallas and whispered in a pained voice, my fear for him palpable, "Viking man." I reached up and cupped his cheek.

"You'll be free, and soon." He nodded more to himself than me. He ran his thumb over my bottom lip before spinning and bolting for the window; Beast was already out.

He climbed through, and my eyes landed on his backside. My nerves momentarily fled, which was how I found myself saying, "Nice arse, Viking man. I'd tap it."

Once his feet were planted, he spun around and growled low,

"Jesus, woman." Though, I saw the smirk playing on his lips before he disappeared in a puff of smoke.

What were they teaching those biker men?

My door crashed opened just after I got the window closed. Jumping, I spun around to find one of Jimmy's new men standing there. His eyes flicked around the room with suspicion.

Pointing to the window, I said, "There was scratching outside. I just saw a dog. Did Jimmy get some dogs? I like dogs. I've always wanted one when I was younger, but I never got one, so I was so excited to see—"

The door slammed as he exited. I had wondered why he'd shown in the first place, but I hoped whatever it had been was lost from his mind.

Moving to the window, I looked out.

Only I did it smiling.

Dallas was in Sydney.

He was there for me.

"He'll help. Even when I said not to because he's stubbornly a pain in my butt."

My regret from not saying anything to him, to the Hawks members and Mason back in Melbourne would always, *always* be present.

But still, hope flared to life.

The heaviness from deep inside of me started to ease, and it was all because of a certain Viking man.

CHAPTER FOUR

MELISSA

*M*y desk at Jimmy's main office was right outside his door and next to his assistant's desk. She was new, young, ditzy, and would probably fall for his charm instantly. Jimmy would make sure she did, like he had everyone in that office. The men adored him, wanted to be him and the women fawned over him, even when they knew I was his wife and worked there also. His workers all sat in their cubicles on the floor vying for his attention when he made an appearance.

It was pathetic and all because he had money and power.

His previous assistant had been fired as soon as she hit twenty. His new one looked fifteen but was actually eighteen, and since he liked to look at them when he walked in and out of his office, she may last a bit longer than most. Not that he'd touch them or anything, even if they were gagging for it. No, he didn't lay a hand on anyone in a sexual way if they were over the age of seventeen.

My stomach rolled at the thought of Jimmy and his actions. He was sick.

Sicker than anyone I'd ever met. Even my father, who used to beat and rape my mother. However, that soon changed when he left, never looking back... not until I found him. Actually, I found his bank balance; it soon dwindled down to nothing when I hacked in and took what was owed to us. Which was how my mum could live comfortably in an apartment on the Gold Coast. He didn't have a clue what had happened because it had stated he'd made the withdrawal himself from his own computer at home. Stupid fucker ended up bankrupt and moving in with his loser father. They deserved to be miserable with each other. My sperm donor's parents had hated my mum and me.

It was lucky my mum did live in the Sunny Coast of Queensland so she couldn't see what a loser I'd turned out to be. She had no clue what I was going through. I had managed to ring her the night I had been handed over to Jimmy and told her I was heading out into no man's land for a while to commune with the spirits. She knew I liked to travel, so she wasn't surprised I was doing it again.

"Morning." Amber's, Jimmy's assistant, cheery voice broke through my thoughts.

Glancing up, I saw two of Jimmy's men on each side of Della. My eyes widened, my belly pivoting when I saw a bruise like my own on her cheek, only mine was covered with a lot of make-up.

As I opened my mouth to speak with her, she shook her head slightly, and I deflated like a balloon. Something had happened, and it was bad enough that she couldn't be seen talking to me at all.

"Mr Vanclove," one of the men barked.

Amber's body jolted into action, picking up the phone and checking if the boss was happy to be seen. She placed the phone back on the desk and said, "He said go right in."

Della looked fearful, and my heart ached for her. She seemed thinner than usual. Her blonde hair was dirty and in a messy bun. Her dress was short, so as she started for the door giving me a small, sad smile, I saw the hand prints on her upper thighs.

They were still abusing her.

Anger burned inside me.

He'd promised me.

He fucking promised.

Jimmy had reassured me if I did all I did for his business, they would leave her alone.

Why had that changed? And for how long had I been blind to think I could trust that man? That motherfucker.

Tears pooled in my eyes as they met her pain-filled blue ones just before the door closed behind them.

"You know, you can still see the bruises no matter how much make-up you use," Amber said, grabbing my attention. "What did you do to deserve them?"

My head jerked back. I sneered, leaning in and bit out through clenched teeth, "I did nothing to deserve them."

She snorted, her look gazing all over me. "Right." She smirked before turning back to her computer. I picked up my paper-weight, wanting to throw it at the back of her head. But decided not to. If she was dumb enough to think people deserved bruises, no matter what happened in the situation, then fuck her and her idiocy.

Instead, I placed it back down with a thump, causing her to jump and look over at me. I gave her the middle finger and shifted my gaze back to my screen. I was supposed to be gaining information on Jimmy's new business client, but I couldn't keep my mind on the work. Not when Della was in his office, not when my thoughts kept running over the possibilities of what could have happened. Had she done something? Said something? I knew I promised her I would get us out of this mess, but I'd also said it would take time. I'd asked her to hold on. Had she'd given up because of the abuse? My naivety made me feel sick. My hand went over my stomach.

God, I *didn't* know.

Abruptly, I stood when a scream tore through the office.

"No," I breathed when a gun shot was let off next. "No, no, no," I chanted frantically as I made my way to the door. My whole body shook in fear.

"You can't go in there," Amber stated.

How in the fuck was everyone so calm after hearing that?

They're all insane.

My heart was in my throat, and with a trembling hand, I reached out for the door when it suddenly came open.

Jimmy stood in it with a smile on his face. "Excuse me, Melissa."

Peering over him, my eyes widened when I spotted Della in the arms of one of Jimmy's men, bridal style.

"What did you do?" I snapped and tried my best to shove past him. He took my arms in his hands, his grip hard. I gasped from the strength he used.

"Turn around now and step aside," he hissed in my ear.

"Jimmy, please—" *You motherfucking prick.*

"Now!"

Turning, his grip loosened and then dropped. Even though everything inside of me wanted to fight him, I moved aside. My hand lifted to the side of my neck and I squeezed. I wanted to throw up, to scream and throw myself at them.

Jimmy stepped out of his doorway and announced, "All is fine. The dear woman heard some bad news and wanted to take her own life. We prevented it. My men are taking her to get some help."

People clapped.

They fucking clapped for him.

Like he was a hero.

I wanted to curse them all.

Couldn't they see what a liar he was? Were they that blind?

Jimmy shifted from the door, and his men stepped out. As they walk towards the lift, I heard people tell them what a good job they did.

Sheep. That was what they were, and Jimmy was the wolf disguised as the ram who they followed.

I wanted to spit on them, snarl in their faces, for what they were doing.

Where were they taking Della? What had happened to bring her in the office? Why did she scream? Why was there a gunshot?

My mind was a swirling pool of thoughts.

And all of them made my heart clench and my body shake in fear.

"Melissa." Jimmy's voice sounded right in my ear. I tensed.

"Mr Vanclove, you have an appointment in ten."

His hand wound around my upper arm and squeezed. "Thank you, Amber. Hold them here until I have a quick word with my wife."

"Your wife?" If I wasn't swimming in dread, I would have laughed at Amber's shock.

"Yes." Jimmy nodded and then steered me into his office, shutting the door behind us.

My feet took me to the seat opposite his desk. As I sat, I saw the bullet hole in his desk. Right in front of where he sat.

Even through my terror for Della, a small smile slipped onto my lips. Just a few inches and it would have hit Jimmy in the dick. Right where he needed it.

Jimmy sighed behind me. I jumped, causing him to chuckle and then walk around his desk to sit and then lean back as he studied me.

I made sure the smile had fallen from my lips before he'd even taken a step. Besides, panic had swarmed once again.

"What are you doing with Della?" I demanded.

He said nothing, but kept looking at me.

"Did she do something?" Was it her who shot off the gun? That was what I really wanted to know.

His lips thinned before he ran a hand over his face.

He looked to his desk, to the hole in it from the bullet. Reaching out, he flicked flecks of timber around the desk. "Della has brought her own trouble."

"How?" I asked in an alarmed high-pitched tone. I needed to know what had happened and what they would do with her.

"She didn't follow the rules."

"Jesus, Jimmy, what rules? What did she do? Why did she scream?"

"I'm afraid you're not going to like the answer." His brow rose, and I fell silent. *No, Della, what did you do?* "Because no matter what, she must die."

I closed my eyes, took a deep breath, and clenched my hands on the armrests. What I didn't do, like I wanted to, was scream and yell and hurt him.

"Why?" my weak voice whispered.

"She killed a client last night."

Anger burst free. Fisting my hand, I leaned forward and punched it onto his desk. "Why was she with a client? *You* said, you *promised* all she had to do was strip, Jimmy. I did as you asked to keep her away from all of your fucked up clients. *Why* was she with one?"

He leaned forward, his eyes narrowing.

I stayed where I was and told him, "You aren't scaring me, Jimmy. You have nothing over me any longer. I was only ever doing as I was told to keep Della safe."

Jesus.

No. Not Della.

Fuck.

Tears pooled in my eyes. I wanted to pick up my chair, throw it at him and run from the room to help Della... but I knew it would be useless. He had men everywhere.

He scoffed. "She wasn't all that I had over you, Melissa. You know this."

Throwing out a hand, I said, "Take what you have on me to the police. So what? I'll go to jail. I don't care, Jimmy."

"You will. Especially when I'll make sure they'll make your life hell in there. You'll be stuck on the inside while I'm out and free and..." He smiled. "...taking good care of your mum."

I froze.

He laughed. "You thought I didn't know about her. Foolish really." He laughed. "You'll keep doing what you are for me, and she'll stay safe. You get past all walls through any system. I'm yet to try out your thieving skills, but I will, one day. You're important to me, Melissa. I won't lose you, and you'll be taken care of as long as you toe the line. Della was nothing. She thought she could fuck with my business, she can't and will now pay the price. No amount of tears or pleading will help her case. She was useless to me, so I see no loss when they've taken care of her."

"You're a monster," I whispered, my heart breaking for Della. Exhaustion held back what I really wanted to do, which was to finish the job Della had tried. Kill him with a bullet to the brain.

He smiled at me. "Thank you."

"You'll be taken down one way or another."

My thoughts ran right to Dallas.

"I highly doubt it."

"Never—"

His phone rang, and his hand came up. I closed my mouth, and he answered, "Yes?" He stood, his chair falling to the floor. "What?" His jaw clenched. "You're fucking kidding me." A pause, and whatever was said over the line made his eye twitch. "Deal with it, or I deal with you." He hung up and threw the phone across the room. It smashed against the door and fell to the floor.

"Jimmy?"

His angry eyes flashed to me.

A hesitant small knock came at the door. "Mr Vanclove."

"It's fine," he snapped and spun to face the window, the room filling with fury.

"Jimmy?"

"Leave," he snarled.

"What happened?" I pressed.

He snorted. "You'll be happy to know Della lives for now."

My heart beat happy and hard in my chest. "How?" I breathed.

My Viking man. I ran a hand over my mouth, hiding my smile and looked to the floor.

"Someone overtook my men and grabbed her." He moved to face me, and I lifted my head to see his eyes were deadly. "I'll find out who, and with her, they will also die."

Anything could be possible, but that.

They wouldn't die.

Dallas had been in town a few hours, as far as I knew, and he'd already rescued Della. She was safe, free. The Hawks men could do anything and I didn't see death in *their* lives. No, not them.

But Jimmy's life was up for the taking, and I knew when the Hawks men set their eyes on something they wanted, they'd make it certain to happen.

How long would Jimmy have left?

I wasn't sure, but I knew I looked forward to when it happened.

CHAPTER FIVE

DALLAS

*A*fter we'd left Melissa's house, I couldn't sleep. We went back to the hotel and I filled my brothers in on everything she'd told me. I'd hated leaving her there. Hated it right down to my core. What I wanted was to rush to the motherfucker's room and take him out. I guess it was luck, and my woman's words, that got me to leave because Knife told me later that ten men arrived at the house. We weren't sure why they'd come. I was furious they'd showed. Spitting mad and stressed as fuck they'd hurt Melissa, I wanted to rush over and pull her out regardless of the fuckin' consequences, but my brothers held me back. It was only Knife's reassurance that she was fine that allowed me to grasp on our need to make plans.

"What's the plan?" Knife asked as soon as I'd finished explaining everything that Melissa had told me.

"Gonna call in more brothers. This fucker needs a lesson and we're gonna teach him. Then, since I know Tiny won't leave until this other chick, Della, is safe, we do our own research, and goddamn quickly, to get her out. Then we get Tiny out."

Knife handled the call to Dodge, while I rang around to the strip clubs looking for a Della.

Five of them said there was no Della. Only one said they had one, but she no longer worked there. Which set off alarms inside of me.

"Beast," I called. "Get on the computer, find out all you can on this dickhead Jimmy Vanclove."

Beast gave me a chin lift, went to the table, and got down to work.

"Sick fucker likes little girls," I mumbled to myself.

"He needs to pay slow-like," Knife said.

Glancing at him, I saw he was off the phone. "We can do slow."

"Fuck yeah we can." He smiled. "You gonna be cool waiting for shit while your woman is under the same roof as him?"

"Yep."

Knife snorted. "She didn't give you a choice, did she?"

Glaring, I said, "No." And I fucking hated it, but Tiny, my Melissa, was right about one thing. The cocksucker needed to be taken down. Then, once it was all over, I'd have her in my arms, in my bed, and under me.

"Should we get some shuteye before the brothers arrive?" Knife asked.

"Can't. Need you at that strip club. They run 24/7. Keep your eyes and ears peeled. Any word about the Della chick, I want to know."

He sent me a wave, got up from the bed, and started for the door. Before he was out it, I called his name. Once I had his eyes, I asked, "Who's coming?"

"Dodge, Handle, Dive, Pick, and Billy."

The ache in my chest eased a little. It wasn't that I didn't trust the three of us to get the job done, but having more brothers at our backs would make sure we all came out of the situation alive.

It was over two hours later, around 4:00 a.m., when my phone rang. I was grateful for the break because Beast and I had been going over shit we'd found on Jimmy Vanclove. The cunt was a billionaire, and he thought he was untouchable. There'd been several cases on him about child porn and kidnapping; all got cleared though. He had many in his back pockets. But I didn't give a flying fuck. He'd soon find out when Hawks had their sights set on something nothing got in our way. We always dealt with shit any way we wanted.

Looking at the caller ID, Knife's name flashed up. "Yo?" I answered.

"Heading back to the hotel. Heard some shit, man, and saw many men shuffling to the back rooms for some reason. I think the woman you're after just caused some shit and she's off to see the bossman in the morning about it. 'Round nine thirty."

"Right, we'll get ready to head here. Won't have the brothers by that time, so the three of us are gonna have our hands full until then. See you when you get back."

After hanging up, I threw my phone on the bed and turned to Beast. "You ready to kick some arse if it comes down to it?" His smile was big.

Yeah, after knowing what the fuckhead liked to do with little girls, we were ready to take Vanclove down a peg in any way we could.

Beast picked up his gun and waved it around. Nodding, I said, "Yeah, man. We're going in fully loaded."

As soon as Knife showed to the hotel, we took off to check the surrounding area around his office building. After some time,

Knife and I were sitting in a coffee shop across from the high-rise block while Beast was out on the streets keeping an eye on his own area. It was 9:00 a.m. when a limousine pulled up out the front. The driver got out and walked around to the back door to open it.

My heart jumped when my eyes landed on Tiny getting out of the car. Her face was caked in make-up, covering her bruising, but I knew what lay beneath and it fucking burned low in my gut. She stood, with a mask of composure on her face, beside the car and waited for fuckface. When he got out my eyes flashed to Knife's; he was already smiling.

"That's the cunt?" he questioned. I nodded and knew exactly what he was thinking. The guy was a pissant, small in height and skinny as fuck. He might have a pricey suit on, but he still looked like a little dweeb. Still, he had armed men around him, all huge fuckers willing to protect him.

Christ, did they know what he liked?

Money probably talked enough for those pricks.

The dick walked to Melissa's side and placed his hand on her back, leading her into the office. I clenched my jaw and fists.

"Hey. We're gonna get this girl for your girl, and then we can get her out," Knife reassured me.

"He has to go down."

"He will." Knife nodded.

"No cops, he dies."

"Done."

"By my hands," I added.

"Agreed."

They entered the building. My legs bounced up and down under the window table. I had to fight myself from jumping up and racing over there to take her. She was made to be at my side and no one else's. Fuck, no woman drove me insane like she had.

It was like she'd switched a light on in my head and heart

about wanting more than just a quick lay. Never thought much of women, until her.

She pushed.

She taunted.

She snuck her way inside of me, and I couldn't let her go.

Never in my whole fucking life did I think I'd succumb to wanting a relationship.

Christ, I wanted to gag on that word.

R-relationship.

But she had, which was why I was there. Since she was the first to open my eyes, to want more than just a bed partner, I had to see if things would be as good as I thought they could be between us.

I wasn't stupid though. I knew she'd piss me off. I knew she'd get on my nerves, but I was willing to try.

For her, I would try.

Fuck me. That was what relationships were about.

"You all right?" Knife asked.

Clearing my throat, I nodded. I hadn't realised I'd actually been flinching over *that* word.

I flicked my eyes to the alleyway beside the building. A van had just pulled in. "Text Beast. I think it's time to party."

Tensing, I saw two men get out of the van. One reached back in and dragged a woman roughly out. She stumbled over to the side door of the building. They tapped in a code and it opened.

"We're gonna catch them on the way out. Don't want to grab the attention of the guards in the lobby. We do this silent. Call Beast, tell him if there're cameras in the alleyway, he needs to cut their feed, but he needs to do it right before we take the woman off their hands so it doesn't draw more attention."

"On it." Knife nodded and then stood from the table, walking out the front.

It wouldn't be long until we put a dint in the motherfucker's life, and soon the dint would turn into a tear. Then I'd rip it wide open.

Smiling, I stood and went to get into position.

My hands twitched at my sides as I waited at the front end of the alley, leaning against the wall and pretending to play on my phone. Beast was down the other end and Knife, after Beast had cut the feed, was in position on the other side of the van. We knew, if they were like Hawks, the meeting wouldn't go long. He'd say what he needed to the woman and then get her out of there.

I heard the side door open and stood tall, slipping my phone into my pocket. I then entered the alley as the side door closed behind them. The woman was passed out or knocked out bridal style in one man's arms. I had to chuckle. The boss dickhead still only had two men with her. Was he fucking stupid?

"Morning, fellas," Knife announced as he stepped around the van. He cocked the free one in the head. The other went to shout and drop the woman, but Beast was there taking her from him while I came sprinting down and taking him to the ground.

With my hand around his neck, I clipped, "Keys."

His eyes flicked to the other man on the ground. Knife rolled him over, grabbed the keys from his pocket, and stood smiling.

"These fools make things too easy."

"Dumb fucks is what they are," I noted, and then punched the guy I straddled in the face. He went lights out. "I'm driving. Beast, you're keeping her while Knife gets in the back with one of these idiots. Leave the other one to call in, letting bossman know his world's about to crumble around him."

Knife easily picked up the one he'd knocked out, while I climbed to my feet and unlocked the van. Once I had the side door opened, Knife threw the guy in the back.

"He's gonna have one hell'va headache." Knife chuckled.

Beast carefully climbed into the back, cradling the woman to him. Fuck, she looked like shit, as if she hadn't eaten in days, and her body held splatters of bruises and cuts in places that made my fury rise.

After Knife got in, I slammed the door closed, kicked the fucker on the ground, and walked around to the driver side.

Soon I'd have my woman.

And soon I'd have more blood on my hands. Only I didn't give one fuck about it.

WHILE KNIFE WAS SECURING the guy in my hotel room to a chair, I helped Beast into their room with the woman. He'd just laid her on the bed, when she gasped awake, sucking in gulps of air hard, causing her whole body to jerk.

She sat quickly, her arms and legs flailing while she gained control over herself. She scooted back on the bed until her back hit the headboard.

"Yo, it's cool. We're good. Calm the fuck down," I tried.

Beast rolled his eyes and shoved me to the side. He sat on the end of the bed and his hand pressed down on thin air in front of her. She watched him closely, her brows drawn down.

"That's Beast. He don't talk." Her fearful eyes came to me. "I'm Dallas. We know Tiny, ah, Melissa." I ran a hand over my head. I was no good at calming a woman down. I was used to riling them up and pissing them off. Scared women freaked the fuck out of me. "Look," I snapped. "We ain't gonna hurt you. We got you away from those fuckers. Relax, woman."

She licked her dry, cracked lips and narrowed her gaze. The woman had balls.

"You got me away for Melissa or for yourselves?"

Screwing up my nose, I said, "I don't fuckin' want you. I got one woman to deal with already." Her gaze went to Beast. I added, "He won't want you either. Now you need to tell us what in the hell went down so we can plan on getting Melissa out."

She studied us for a while and then, fuck, her whole body sagged with relief. "I'm really out?"

Beast nodded. I said, "Yeah."

She sniffed. Ah fuck, was she gonna cry? If she did, I was out of that room like my jocks were on fire.

"Hey," I called. "We need to know everything you do. That Vanclove guy is gonna be pissed you're taken, but at least he ain't holding you over Melis—"

She bounded up to her knees, her hands out. "Wait. They know about her mum. He'll go for her to stop Melissa from leaving. He said as much to me in the office. His men... they were supposed to kill me. Jimmy knew he'd need a backup plan, someone to hang over her head for Melissa to comply with whatever he demanded. You have to save her mum."

"Fuck," I bit out. "You know where she is? Her name?"

She deflated and shook her head. "No, Melissa never really spoke about her mum."

"Shit. Beast, text Julian, see if he knows. If not, get a brother on it at home. We'll take care of it." There was a knock at the door. Beast got up to answer.

When the door swung open, a voice boomed, "Who's ready to party?" Grinning, I walked over to greet Dive who'd entered first.

Then Pick, Billy, Dodge, and Handle. "Fuck, it's good to have you all here."

"Good to be here to help," Dodge said.

"We got a plan yet?" Pick asked.

With a shake of my head, I said, "Not yet." I gestured my head towards Della. "Just about to talk to Tiny's woman."

"You already got her. What fun are we gonna have?" Billy asked.

39

"Don't worry, there's plenty more to come."

"Y-you're all going after Jimmy?" Della's voice quivered. Wasn't sure why her voice shook; wondered if it was because she wasn't feeling safe any longer with a room full of bikers. That, or if she was surprised we'd do such a thing by wading into Tiny's problem.

"Yeah, we are."

"Why?"

"Melissa belongs to me, means she's a part of Hawks. No one fucks with Hawks."

Her body stiffened, her chin jutting up and out. Her eyes went hard before she demanded, "I want to come."

"This ain't women's business."

"Don't let Melissa hear you say that shit," Dodge said with a laugh.

Christ. He was right. My Tiny would have my balls. Not that I'd mind her handling my balls, but she'd be pissed if I didn't let her friend have her two bob on the situation.

Running a frustrated hand over my face, I said, "Look. The situation ain't gonna be a good one. People will die, things will be dangerous. You just got out of a bad situation. You shouldn't want to jump into another one and risk your life."

Her jaw clenched before she hissed out, "My life is mine to do with what I want. For too long I've had my choices taken from me. I've been beaten, raped, and told what to do. I want to come. I have to see that bastard's life end. He took my sister away from me, took her life. I *need* to see his end."

I glanced around to the brothers. They were on board if I was.

Shit. Even though I hated the idea, I found myself surprised by the respect I'd felt for her sticking up for herself in front of us all.

"Fine. Handle," I called. He stepped up. Looking at Della, I ordered, "You stay close to him."

"I will."

Sighing, I said, "Someone find her some proper clothes." My phone chimed with a text from Beast. I smiled. "Looks like the fucker was pissed enough to leave work. Bet he's goin' home and Melissa is with him. The sooner we move out, the sooner we can end this and get the fuck home."

With Tiny with us.

CHAPTER SIX

MELISSA

Jimmy didn't want to stay at the offices for the rest of the day. If I had known what would happen back at the house, I would have begged to have stayed and worked. When we arrived, there were five men already inside. One was Tate, who stood near the bar. He gave me a grim look. Another guy I didn't know sat on the couch in the living room with a cold pack on his face. He straightened when Jimmy and I entered, fear present in his eyes as Jimmy stopped right in front of him.

"Tell me who they were," Jimmy demanded.

"No one I knew, but they did have vests on them."

Smiling and doing the jig was out of option; instead, I schooled my features into a bored expression and looked at my nails.

"Vests?" Jimmy tensed.

The guy nodded and then winced. "Yeah, biker vests."

Through clenched teeth, Jimmy bit out, "Did you catch the name on the vests?"

"Didn't get a chance. They came in fast and took us out. I had mentioned there should have been more men."

It was fast.

I didn't see it coming, so neither did he.

Jimmy pulled a gun out and shot the man between the eyes. Blood sprayed everywhere. I screamed and tried to run from the room, but two men grabbed me.

"Be calm," Tate whispered into my ear, but I couldn't be calm. I saw the man's brains on the wall behind him.

"Shut up!" Jimmy yelled.

Gulping back my emotions, I shook as Tate and the other man held me to my feet. If they hadn't had me in a firm grip, I would have been a pile on the floor.

Jimmy had just shot someone.

Between the eyes.

In front of me.

Blood. So much blood.

Leaning forward, I gagged.

Jimmy was in my face, his hand connecting with my cheek. Pain radiated through my face. "Get yourself together," he ordered.

Closing my eyes, I nodded and took in a deep breath, only to regret it when the coppery scent of blood filled my nose. I clenched my teeth together, straightened, and opened my eye. While my stomach rolled and I felt bile in my throat, I stood tall, shrugging off the men's hold and glared at Jimmy.

He turned and snapped, "Fucking useless prick." He stepped up and kicked the dead guy's leg. "I want the feed from the alley. Marshal is taking too long. Melissa, sit down"—he pointed to a chair not far from the dead guy—"and get me the goddamn fucking feed. I want to know who these bikers are, and I want them to know they can't mess with me."

"Can I at least go into the kitchen?"

"No." He stalked over to me, grabbed me by my hair, and dragged me to the chair, pushing me into it.

I bit back my frustrated anger and picked up the laptop in front of me, before sitting back, avoiding the dead man to my left.

While I worked on the computer, Jimmy paced the room, talking and yelling at his men about how stupid they all were.

Putting the room to the back of my mind, which was something I could always do when I worked, I flew through the system—one I'd designed for him—and pulled up the recorded footage of that morning in the alley. As I watched it, I noticed right away the jolt in the film. I smiled. It meant one of the Hawks men put the video on a loop. We had nothing.

Jimmy wasn't going to like it.

Did I care? No.

"They messed with the camera in the alley and put it on a loop. We have nothing on who they were. We don't even have you guys arriving with Della."

My whole body relaxed in relief.

What I thought would happen was for Jimmy to fly off the deep end by screaming and ranting, so when he just stood there and stared at me, my heart picked up in a double-time pace.

"You knew them," he stated.

Fuck!

Snorting, I placed the computer down and said, "How could I know some bikers?" I folded my arms over my chest and gave him a raised brow.

"Boss, I watched her the whole time she was away. She didn't approach a biker," Tate said. I hadn't known he'd followed me and now he was lying for me.

44

Jimmy ignored Tate and asked, "Who was that friend you saw again?"

"Julian?" I laughed. "I told you he's as gay as they come."

"What was the problem you had to fix for him?"

Yes, Jimmy had been stupid enough to not ask anything more once I told him Julian was an old friend who was gay. Then again, since he had Tate following me, Tate would have told Jimmy something, but what?

Shit, I wasn't sure if what I said would be the right thing. Still, I had to try.

I caught Tate's shake of his head out the corner of my eyes. Licking my suddenly dry lips, I said, "Ah, his parents were giving him shit about being gay, and he wanted help to humiliate them."

Jimmy's eyes narrowed. My pulse jumped and raced as he came slowly my way. Leaning over me, I pulled my head back, to look up at him.

"You're lying to me."

"I'm not."

He studied my face. His hand went around my neck where he tightened his grip. "What was the problem you had to fix for him?"

"H-his parents," I gasped out and gripped his wrist, trying to pull it away from my throat.

"Boss," Tate tried and took a step towards us, only to stop when Jimmy looked to him.

With his face back in mine, he spat, "Try again, what problem did you fix when you were away?"

A throat cleared. Guns were drawn and cocked, the room filled with eight bikers and Della.

Oh God. Della was with them? Why did they bring her? She shook as she stood close to a biker with a beard and tattoos over his arms. I didn't know his name.

"That would be us. She fixed a problem for us." Dallas's smirk was sinister. "And now we're fixing her problem."

Jimmy straightened, grabbed my arm and hauled me up in front of him. "Where are my men?"

Pick snorted. "You mean the pussies outside? All taken out, and looks like you got a problem on the inside as well." He lifted his chin to the dead man on the couch.

"What do you want with my wife?" Jimmy asked, ignoring the comment about his men.

"She's not your wife. She's mine. You forced her to marry you by threatening her people. We don't take to threats well," Dallas said. His eyes flicked to one of Jimmy's men. "Move again, I'll have my brothers kill you."

"You can't just come in here shooting the place down," Jimmy commanded.

Dodge laughed. "You're wrong. We can and we will. All you gotta do is hand her over to us and we'll leave."

That was a lie and I knew it. They wouldn't allow a man like Jimmy who prayed on young girls to live.

Jimmy sneered. "No fucking chance."

"I guess we're in a standoff then, 'cause we ain't leavin' without Dallas's woman." Billy smiled. He had his gun pointed on Tate.

Jimmy pulled his gun around and pressed it against my temple. "I doubt you'll want to damage poor Melissa. Let me walk freely from this room with her and I'll let her go once I am safely away."

"No," Dallas clipped.

Jimmy cocked his gun. "Yes."

"You won't harm her," Della said.

Jimmy turned his glare to her. "Sorry to see you're still living, Mardella. It won't last, I—"

"Fuckin' enough," Dallas boomed. "I ain't here to have a

goddamn tea party and talk shit out. Hand Melissa over and die quickly or let it run its course and die slowly. Which is it?"

My Viking man, never a patient man.

"Things go my way in my house. No doubt I have more men coming my way." One of Jimmy's men nodded. "So you see, soon you'll be surrounded—"

A gun blasted.

Jimmy screamed and released me, dropping to his knees. I jumped sideways and landed on the chair, closing my eyes, but not before I saw the bearded biker taking a gun from Della.

"Don't kill Tate," I screamed, and clenched my eyes tighter.

"Who in the fuck is Tate?" Dallas called out as another gun went off.

"Hope it's not the one I just shot," Dive said.

"Me," Tate called.

"Right, brothers."

More shots rang out through the living room. I buried my head in my arms and curled my legs up. People dropped, things broke, and men screamed.

Please don't let Dallas get shot. Please.

Silence.

The room fell into it.

"Tiny." His tone was gentle. I opened my eyes to see Dallas crouching beside the chair. "Darlin', we gotta go."

"You came." I blinked.

"Yeah, woman."

Launching out of the chair, I threw myself at him. He caught me and stood tall, wrapping his arm around my body. My feet weren't on the ground as he held me tightly, but I didn't care. I knew Jimmy and his men were dead, it was weird how pleased I was over the fact, but all that mattered then was being in Dallas's arms and knowing he, with his brothers, were the ones to save my arse.

My problem was over.

I was free.

And just knowing it had me smiling, my heart warming and my body relaxing.

As Dallas carried me from the room, I heard Dodge say, "Make sure we leave no trace behind. You're comin' with us."

Out the front, I stiffened in Dallas's arms and asked, "Della? Everyone?"

"She's good. Handle got her out after she shot that fucker in the foot, and my brothers are all good."

"Great," I replied and kissed his neck. It was the first time I'd touched my lips to him. Nothing had felt more right.

"Dallas," Dodge called. Dallas planted me on my feet, but hooked his arm around my shoulders, turning us to see Tate was with Dodge as they made their way over. "She's gotta go shopping."

"What?" Dallas barked.

"She needs to be seen on cameras that she's been out shopping, havin' a good time. Tate will take her. Get a story together. They went to lunch first, like she left right after walking out with Jimmy, lunch at a place with no cameras near. Got Beast looking into it."

"I don't trust him—" Dallas started in a harsh tone, only to stop when I touched him.

With a hand on Dallas's chest, I looked up to him and said, "He's fine. I promise. I trust Tate."

He clenched his jaw, his eyes flicking all over my face. Finally, he nodded. After he had made sure we had the address to the hotel, he pulled me against him and kissed me hard. It hurt, from the bruising on my face, but I wouldn't have it any other way. I took notice of the feel of his lips, the teasing touches of his tongue playing with mine. The way his hands were first gripping my shoulders to him, only to slide down to my arse, forcing my body closer to his.

Every movement, every extra racing beat to my heart was locked into my mind because right then, nothing could top it. After all, it was our first shared kiss.

CHAPTER SEVEN

DALLAS

*P*acing the small hotel room, I fisted my hands once again and looked at the clock on the bedside table. She'd been gone for over three hours. Where in the hell was she? My brothers were spread out into other rooms, since the event at the hotel had ended yesterday. Still, the hotel was fairly busy, leaving Beast and Knife to share once again, not that they got to use it from being up all night. Before we'd left to get Tiny, Knife had taken care of the man we'd brought back with us, after questioning him. The idiot knew nothing, but working for a sick fuck still cost him his life.

Some would say we shouldn't have been the ones to deal out a punishment like that. Could even call us cold bastards for what we did. I called it karma. If people wanted to play alongside men like Jimmy Vanclove, then they deserved what they got dealt. My blood hadn't cooled since seeing the fucker Jimmy dead on the floor, if anything I was pissed he hadn't suffered longer, for days in fact. At least on the bright side, my woman could find her peace knowing the sick dick was dead.

When the door opened, I spun to face it. Dodge came in first, then the man named Tate and finally, fucking finally, Tiny.

My eyes narrowed. She looked exhausted. "Where you been?" I demanded.

The prick Tate stepped in front of her and crossed his arms over his chest. I didn't like that one bit. I was in his face in a second, my hand around his throat and I had him backing into a wall. Melissa let out a startled cry. I got close to his face and snarled low, "You get in front of my woman, keep her from me again, and you'll pay."

"Dallas!" Melissa snapped. I heard her small feet stomping my way, while I looked at the man in front of me turning blue. A small hand hit my back. "Don't be a dick. He's helped me all day. He doesn't know you're a snarling Viking freak from the old days and that I can take anything you dish out."

Sighing, I glanced over my shoulder. Shit, my woman was tiny; the top of her head just touched my shoulder.

"I swear, if you don't let him go, I'm going to beat the shit out of you." She glared.

Fighting not to laugh, I released my hold and stepped back, taking Melissa with me and circling my arms around her.

Fuck, it felt good to hold her.

"You're free," I whispered.

She relaxed against me. "I am."

"And you're back to being a shrew with me."

She giggled. "Only because you're being a dick."

"Man, hate to be the bearer of bad news, but we gotta talk," Dodge said. Meeting his gaze, I saw he was relaxing back on the bed, seeming unaffected by my reaction. I had no doubt though that if my woman hadn't claimed me, he would have waded in. Probably.

I tensed. "Wait, what bad news?"

"Melissa?" Dodge said.

Looking back to Tiny, I saw her sigh and nod. She met my gaze after taking a step back. "I presume since you came here for me, you'd want me back in Melbourne with you?"

"Yes," I agreed.

"I would have liked it also, but after hours of speaking to the police and then Tate"—my eyes narrowed and she rolled hers —"we realise it would be too suspicious to go anywhere. When I went home, I rang the police and acted like it was a home intrusion. So far, they don't think I had anything to do with—"

"You don't anyway, it was us."

"Yes, but you came into town for me. To help me. If I move now, go to Melbourne, they end up looking at you all. I can't have that. So I need to stay for a while. Besides, apparently my name is on his business and house, meaning I now own both. I have to get things in order before I up and move." She appeared as surprised as I was at that revelation.

"How long we talkin'?"

She bit her bottom lip. "We think at least eight months."

"Eight fuckin' months?" I boomed.

"Yes." She nodded, her arms crossing her chest.

"Fine, I'll stay and—"

"No," Dodge said.

Spinning to face him, I glared. "What the hell you mean by sayin' no?"

Dodge sat forward. "You stayin' could fuck things up. It's risky her being here right now, but I knew you'd have to hear from her she was good. You can't be seen with her. You'll be coming back with us tomorrow."

"Like fuck. What would you do if it was Low?"

He rose a brow. "I'd do what she wanted because, in the end, I'd realise it could be my arse on the line. Not only that but my brothers'." He stood. "We got your woman outta her shit. She's safe. You need to let her deal with the rest so no blowback comes to us for havin' her back."

I clenched my jaw. I bloody hated when another person was right.

"Fuck," I clipped and ran a hand through my hair.

"Tate's proven himself to protect her."

"Because he wants in her fuckin' panties," I snarled and glared at the offending fucker. The dick smirked back. I went for him until Tiny stood in my way.

She shoved me back, well tried, her small hands didn't budge me. "Stop being a dick. He may have wanted in my panties—" She looked over her shoulder to him. "—not saying you did."

"Oh, I did," he stated.

Dodge groaned.

Melissa sighed while I placed my hands on Melissa's shoulders and gently manoeuvred her aside. She was like a little rabbit and jumped back in front of me. "Hey," she yelled. "He said *did*. Past tense. Besides, it's not like I'd let him in there. Not when *I'll* be waiting for you."

"Relax, man. I'm messing with you. I wouldn't do anything she didn't want," Tate said and smiled. The shit didn't know when to stop.

"And," Melissa yelled, grabbing my attention again, "I won't want anything, so stop being a dick. We have a few hours left with each other. Are you going to spend it killing the only person who's staying and I trust?"

Biting down, I said through clenched teeth, "Killing him could be fun."

"Well, I can think of better things that would be fun."

"Right." Dodge clapped. "That's our cue to go." He walked over to Tate, grabbed him by the back of the neck, and led him out the door.

As soon as the door closed behind them, I glanced to Melissa in time to see her jump at me. A grin broke out over my face as I wrapped my arms around her while she did the same to me, her legs tightening around my waist.

"So, you do like me." Her smile was a cheeky one.

One I kissed away. If that didn't state enough of how much I liked her, then I wasn't sure what could…. Unless we got naked.

Her head titled to the side, her hands gripped my hair, and she turned the kiss into a hungry one. Our lips moulded together while our tongues tangled with one another in an urgent frenzy. Walking backwards, I waited until my legs hit the edge of the mattress and then sat with her in my lap.

I took my hands from her arse to thread them into her hair, where I tightened my grip enough for her to moan against my mouth. I tugged her head back, breaking the kiss. Our heavy breaths panted together. I dove in and sank my teeth into her neck and sucked. She cried out, and I smiled against her skin.

"You mine?" I asked.

"Um."

Lifting my head, I stared her down and asked in a rough tone, "Tiny, are you mine?"

"Well, it's just starting—"

"Fuck it, you're mine, and that's it. We do this, a…" I cleared my throat, to prevent the gag reflex over the next word. "…relationship, see where it goes. But in doing this, us, it *does* goddamn mean you're mine and no one else's."

She rolled her eyes. "Fine, Viking man." Her lips twitched. "But only if you purr the word relationship again."

I snorted and shook my head at my funny-as-fuck woman. The smartarse had seen how I nearly choked on the word. Leaning in, I bit her bottom lip and hissed, "Get stuffed."

I pulled back to see her tap her chin with a finger. "I can think of one thing I'd like to get stuffed with."

"Right." I stood, turned, and threw her arse to the bed. "Lie on your belly."

"Are you going blind in your old age? I'm fully clothed." She ran her hands down over her breasts and stomach.

With a hand to the bed, I bent over her and encased her entire throat with my hand, applying pressure. Her eyes widened, then hooded with heat burning inside of them. My cock hardened from seeing my woman liking a little rough play.

I licked across her lips and ordered, "Lie on your belly." Letting go, I stood tall and crossed my arms over my chest, waiting.

"I don't—"

"Not another word," I demanded gruffly.

She glared but did as she was told, which I'd reward her for. She sat up, got to her knees and then crawled into the middle of the bed where she lay flat on her stomach, her head turned towards me.

"Good girl." I nodded and dropped my arms to my sides. She looked perfect lying on the bed. Fisting my hands, I took a breath and climbed over her. Sitting on her arse, I ran my hands up and down her back, gently massaging my fingers in. Her eyes closed, her mouth opened a little. As I ran my hands down again, I gripped the bottom of her tee and pulled it up, she lifted enough so I could get the tee free and throw it to the floor. Unhooking her bra, I dug my fingers into her muscles again. Tiny hummed under her breath.

I flicked her hair to the side and bent to take her earlobe into my mouth where I sucked and then bit.

"You gonna do as I say?" I asked.

She nodded.

Slowly, I kissed and bit her neck, her shoulder, her back and then lower. She wiggled against the bed. "Do not move or I stop," I told her.

I smiled when I saw her clamp down on her bottom lip. She wanted to say something, she itched to, but she didn't because she wanted this, me, more.

Pressing my lips to her skin just above the waistline of her leggings, I licked from left to right, then jerked her leggings and panties down over her arse.

"Fuck," I bit out. Her arse was round and stunning. I palmed each cheek, and she sighed when I leaned in and said, "No one will ever touch you again but me. Only when I do it you'll love every fuckin' second." Moving down her body on my knees, I pulled her leggings with me. With a finger, I glided it over her crease of her arse and then down between her legs, curling a finger up and inside of her. She moaned, and I hissed out a breath when I found her soaked.

"From how wet you are, I can tell you like me also," I commented before I kissed her arse cheek.

"Maybe, but—"

My hand landed on her arse hard. "Did I say you could talk?"

Her jaw clenched after she snapped her mouth closed. Her eyes told me, as she looked over her shoulder again, that she wanted to kill me, but she stayed put.

"Yeah, you like me." I smiled, rubbed her arse and then dipped my finger back inside of her. I wanted more room though, so I ordered, "Spread them." She did, and I placed my knees between her legs. The leggings restricted movement, and her pointed look at them told me as much also. "They digging into your legs, Tiny?" She nodded. I grinned. "Good. Want you to feel the pain when you leave later. Want you to feel me in a lot of places when I've gone. Fuckin' sucks we only get each other once. But I want what I do to you to linger so deep, you're gonna find it so fuckin' hard to forget me."

I watched the pulse in her neck pick up speed. She liked the thought of me lingering on her. Leaning down, I bit her arse and then sucked her skin into my mouth. She moaned. I did it over and over until not only her arse but her back and then shoulders had my mark on her. I only wished it'd last eight goddamn months.

As I licked back down her back, I sank a finger right into her and never thought it possible she'd be wetter for me. "Primed just for me. Fuckin' perfect." I pumped my finger in and out of her, her mouth opened in a silent moan, her eyes closed tight. She was close.

Removing my finger, she grumbled under her breath in complaint.

"You don't come yet," I told her. If she held off, I knew the tension would build and I wanted her to come hard. On my knees, I threw my tee off and undid the top button of my jeans. Grabbing my wallet, I took out a condom, placed it between my lips, all while my woman watched. My hand went back to my jeans, where I slowly unzipped and then shoved them down. As I palmed myself with one hand, the other I used to take the condom and tear it open with my teeth. Sliding it on, I asked, "You want my cock?"

She nodded. Laying my body over hers, I pushed my hand over her neck and surrounded it in my large hand. I used the other to grab my hard dick. "Lift a little," I ordered. She did. I played with my knob against her opening right before I tightened my grip around her throat and slammed deep inside of her. She cried out. I lessened my grip so she could get her breath back in. With my other hand on the bed, I straightened my arm out, so I was hovering over her while I slowly pulled back out. She whimpered, wanting my cock back, so I gave it to her and thrust all the way back in.

I dug my feet into the bed and lay back over her, and gave her my weight so I could use my feet to lift up and continue to fuck her while my grip around her neck squeezed.

I did it until she turned red.

"Christ." I groaned. I loosened my hand, and she sucked in a big breath. "Stunning." Removing my hand altogether, I got to my hands and demanded, "Get on your knees, but do not lose me from within you."

Slowly, she climbed to her knees. I nearly slipped all the way out, if she hadn't backed onto me. With my hands on her hips, I fucked her hard. She whimpered and moaned, her hand taking hold of her breast.

She was mine.

Fucking mine. I was pissed we only had a short amount of time to appreciate one another. I was a selfish bastard, so I knew when she moved my way, I'd have all her time, attention whenever I wanted it. And knowing the way I was feeling, I'd want it a lot.

Sliding one hand around, I played with her clit. "Say my name," I said harshly.

"Dallas," she cried out, her head thrown back.

"Who's inside of you?"

"My Viking man."

"Yeah, fuck yeah I am. This pussy is mine. You're mine."

"Yes," she screamed as her walls contracted around my cock.

I took the opportunity to spit on my finger and slip it into her arse. She was tight, but she was lost in her orgasm, so she didn't care. She yelled, still coming, and pushed back against my cock and finger.

"Jesus," I gritted through clenched teeth. "You feel me?"

"God, yes."

"Good." I groaned as I exploded inside of her.

She collapsed to the bed panting. I fell next to her, my eyes on her face, waiting to see if she didn't like anything I did. She opened her eyes and smiled at me.

My heart hammered in my chest.

Beautiful.

Leaning in, I kissed her once. "You got five minutes to rest. I wanna eat your pussy and mark your tits with my mouth."

"I'm not sure—"

"Eight months, Tiny."

Her eyes warmed. "Whatever you want, Viking man, because I'm going to miss you too."

CHAPTER EIGHT

MELISSA

*J*ust hours with Dallas Gan wasn't enough. I wished I could have stayed in bed with him, curled up with his warmth and attitude. He didn't want me to go as much as I didn't want to leave. But I had to, to keep him and his brothers out of the police's notice.

Tate drove as I sat in the passenger seat gazing out the window. My heart hurt. I hadn't known Dallas long, but he'd made an imprint on my life, one I liked. He was rough, mean and yet, since the first time I'd seen him, I couldn't get him out of my mind.

Because he was mine.

Made for me.

He'd saved me, cared about me when others didn't.

"Are you sure you want to be involved with the Hawks MC?" Tate asked.

My gaze swung to him. "I'm not being a bitch here to you,

Tate. However, please don't question my involvement with the Hawks since they were the ones who saved my arse." His jaw clenched, his nostrils flaring. I laid a hand on his arm and added, "I know you would have tried, but you're *one* man against many. I didn't want to risk your life for mine and Della's."

"I should have done—"

"No. You did what you could. Thank you for having my back when I needed it the most." I took my hand from his arm after a squeeze and placed it over the burner phone in my lap that Beast had given me as I was leaving. "Do you think you can help me get... things under control with the business?"

"Of course."

"What about Jimmy's other men?"

"There are a few I trust. The rest we'll have to let go if they don't follow the line."

"If they don't?" I asked.

"Then we get rid of them any way possible. However, the worst were in that room with Jimmy, so the others should be easier to control."

"Do you...?" I bit my bottom lip and flicked my gaze to the windscreen, then back to Tate.

"What?" he asked.

"Do you want to stay? Jimmy's no longer around. It means you don't have to be either. Whatever he held over you is gone. I would never—"

"I know you wouldn't. And what he had over me was a gambling debt, but that was paid off a while ago. I stayed to keep an eye on you."

His admittance clenched my stomach.

"Don't," he ordered.

"Don't what?" I whispered.

"At first I wanted you for myself. It's changed now. I protect you as I would my own sister, if I had one. I know you and that

Hawks guy have something going on. I won't do shit to stuff things up for you. It's time to be happy."

I wasn't sure if he was calling the sister card just to make me feel better. I honestly didn't want him sticking around if he thought there could be something between the two of us. So I asked, "Can you be happy, Tate?"

He smiled. "I think I can, given time."

"I hope so."

We pulled into the hotel near the house. There was no way I would step foot in the house until it had been cleared out. It had been bad enough going back into it when I had to ring the police. I wished I had the ability to read minds when I'd been questioned. I was sure they suspected me, even when they said I wasn't on the list. From the looks they gave each other, I reckoned they'd just said that to be nice and I'd be the biggest suspect out of anyone.

At least I knew if they dug for dirt on myself or Jimmy, they wouldn't find anything. Not since I was the one who designed the program on all his computers. I sent what dirt I had to Julian's and made sure it showed in his junk file since I knew he never checked that folder. Then I cleaned all personal computers completely with the laptop I'd taken from the house in between visiting shops for my alibi.

When the detective had entered and asked me all the questions the cops had, I'd held back my groan and told him the same things. The bruises on my face were from the private ju-jitsu lessons Tate was giving me under Jimmy's orders because he'd been acting paranoid that someone was following him for some time. But other than that, Jimmy and I had been so much in love that I worked in his offices as well. I mentioned how he'd saved my friend Della from becoming an addict and how freaked out I'd been about learning of her drug use. There were too many witnesses in the office who saw Della being carried out and how I reacted.

Della had already been sent to the hotel I was staying in. I'd made sure to get a double room. I think what we both needed was time with each other.

Tate walked me to my door. I gave him a quick hug and unlocked it using the key I had from checking in before I'd snuck out and went to Dallas.

I found Della sitting on the bed closest to the bathroom. She was in the new clothes I'd purchased while out shopping, a tee and some sleep shorts. Her hair was wet from a shower and when she looked over at me, her eyes filled with tears.

Nodding, I made my way to the bed, my own eyes misting. Sitting next to her, I pulled Della into my arms. "I'm so sorry."

"Please, don't," she whispered into my hair. "I know you did what you could. I'm sorry for stuffing things up and… and nearly getting myself killed."

Shifting back, I cupped her cheek and told her, "I would have done the same." Shaking my head, I grabbed hold of her hands with mine and rested them on her leg. "No, that's not true. I wouldn't have been as strong as you. I would have done something a long time ago. What they did, what you put up with, I couldn't have done it."

"It's over now."

My lips turned up a little in a sad smile because I knew, deep down her nightmare wouldn't be over in her mind. I said, "It is."

She sucked in a deep breath through her nose and nodded. With her eyes to the bed, she said, "I think I need to see my parents." As far as they knew, she'd taken off after her sister's death because she couldn't deal. They had no clue she'd been trying all along to bring her sister justice.

"It's a good idea."

She looked up at me. Fear pulled her brows down. "Will you come with me?"

I wrapped an arm around her shoulders and replied, "Of course I will."

"You don't go anywhere without me," a new, deeper voice said.

I screamed, flailing my arms in the air as I jumped from the bed and stood in front of Della. "What in the fuck?" I yelled at the bearded guy in the corner of the room.

A knock came at the door. "Melissa, you okay in there?"

"Yeah," I called and made my way over to the door. Opening it, the bearded guy stood as Tate entered.

"What's going on?" Tate asked. He took in the man, me, and then Della still sitting on the bed.

Della threw a hand out towards the guy. "I should have warned Melissa I had a guard. He surprised her is all. I just forgot he was even in the room." She glared over at him. "He's easy to forget."

"Um," I started, but for the life of me I couldn't remember his name. I think it had something to do with a bike though. Horn? Helmet?

"Name's Handle."

Right, Handle.

Tate shook Handle's hand and stepped back. "I thought all you were leaving?" he asked.

"I was asked to stay on for Della's protection."

"And I kept saying I didn't need protecting," Della snapped from the bed, glaring at Handle.

He glared back. "Until we're sure, then I follow orders."

"Ah, I'm going to head back to my room." Tate quickly gave me a smile and fled the room like it was on fire, leaving me in an awkward situation.

Della let out a frustrated breath. "There is no one who would come for me now. It's pointless you being here. You're wasting time where you could be home doing whatever you're supposed to be doing."

When Handle said nothing, just crossed his arms over his chest and sat back in the chair, Della threw her hands up in the air and growled under her breath. She looked to me. "Can you do anything?"

My head jerked back. "What do you want me to do?"

"You're dating one of them. Tell whoever you need to and get him to back the hell off. I don't need yet another male in my personal space again."

Her eyes dropped to the bed, her chest rising and falling rapidly. Understanding dawned. She was over men telling her what to do. She wanted her life back, and after what she'd been through, it was highly likely she didn't want anything, not one single thing, to do with the opposite sex.

Having Handle around wanting to protect her was no doubt confusing her since all she knew for some time was abuse by men.

Sitting back on the bed next to her, I suggested, "Why don't we just give it a few days. I'm sure he won't be too much of a bother." Glancing to Handle, I asked, "You're not sleeping in here, right?"

"No. Next room, but I wanted to be in here until you got here."

"Okay." I nodded. Picking up Della's hand, I said, "From what I've gathered, and I'm sure you can see yourself, Hawks men are protective. They just got us out of one situation, and they don't want to risk us for another—" I held up my hand when she went to talk. "—if one were to occur. We aren't sure all of Jimmy's men will be okay with the shift in business and owners. They know you mean something to me, people could use that to take the business from under me." I shrugged. "Just for a little while, will you let Handle stick around?"

"Yes," she whispered. Her watery eyes flicked from the bed, to me, and then to Handle. "But he doesn't need to be in here while you're with me."

"No, he doesn't."

"I stayed to answer any questions."

"I have a question," I piped up. "Why were you picked to stay and not Dallas?"

His hard eyes softened, but only a little. Handle held a darkness inside of him. His unsmiling face and cold eyes told me that. "If Dallas had stayed, it would be too difficult to explain why he's around you all the time and why you'd be sharing a bed if you're being watched by the police. I can be explained. If anyone asks who I am, I'm an old boyfriend of Della's. We've rekindled our relationship."

That was true. If Dallas had stayed, I wouldn't have helped myself and had him close to my side, which could have led me in more trouble with the police.

"Don't worry. He was pissed he didn't get picked to stay."

I snorted. "That I believe."

Handle stood and walked to the door. "Inform me if either of you are leaving the room. My mobile number is on the bedside table."

"Thank you," I managed to get out before he walked out with a grunt. Sighing, I said to Della, "They can be pretty full on."

It was her turn to snort and then smile. "You think?" Her expression sobered. "At first, they freaked me out when I woke. They explained you meant something to them, especially Dallas. Then they made plans to get you out. Being with them, seeing what they could do…. Melissa, they killed his men without even making a sound." She shook her head and then added quietly, "I think they scare me more than Jimmy and his men. Only that doesn't make sense because I also know, just with how they were with me, they don't condone treating women the way we've been treated."

Smiling gently, I offered, "They're confusing, hard, gruff, but they'll do anything for people they know. My friend Julian, who is over-the-top gay, has been around them for years now and they accepted him because his sister-in-law is married to their president. They knew I was Julian's friend and I was welcomed with open arms. Once you've been accepted by them, you enter their world and circle of trust, love, and protection. All I can say is that, in a way, even though they're scary, they're amazing men." A pang of loss hit me square in the chest. Talking about them meant Dallas popped into my mind and the sudden emotion hit me, knowing he wasn't close. I clenched my jaw. I didn't want Della to see the raw emotion I felt. Instead, I hid it behind a fake smile.

Della nodded. "I can see that, but I can't turn off being paranoid and wait for the other shoe to drop with them... well, Handle at least. Maybe in time, but I don't know."

"It's okay. I understand. Besides, once he knows nothing is going to happen since Tate will be at my side helping me, he'll back off and fly home. For now, let's organise when you want to see your parents."

Shaking her head, she said, "I'm not ready just yet, maybe next week. I just want time to myself for a while."

"Okay. So for now, we'll stay here until the house is clean then you can move in there with me, and if you want, if you get bored, you can help me work out what I'm going to do with Jimmy's businesses." I felt I had to be brave, act strong for Della, when on the inside, I wished my Viking man was there.

"I can do that." She smiled, then leaned in and hugged me. "Thank you, for always being there and helping me."

"Ditto."

CHAPTER NINE

MELISSA

*a*fter three weeks, I'd soon discovered the phone calls to Dallas weren't enough. I missed the big idiot a lot. His scent, his body, his attitude... every last lickable part of him. At least I got to hear his voice most nights, but I was a greedy bitch and wanted all of him.

I was being emotional. Though not all the emotions had to do with missing Dallas. After two weeks of headaches with the business, I appointed Tate as CEO. I wasn't cut out for the corporate world. I liked messing with computers too much. Tate had a few close friends within Jimmy's crew, and he picked them to help him get things smoothed out within the workforce. To my surprise, the men who I thought were loyal to Jimmy and would have kicked up a fit over the change and Jimmy's death didn't. As long as they got paid, they didn't give a shit who was in charge. In fact, Tate had told me they were happy with Jimmy finally pushing daisies. They thought him a sick and twisted motherfucker, but he was one who paid well. Then again, Jimmy's most loyal men had died alongside him that day, so perhaps it wasn't such a surprise.

Of course, I fired Jimmy's old assistant Amber and hired Tate a new one. A woman I actually liked. She was in her late twenties, had attitude, and could work under pressure. She was perfect, and what was also great was the fact she was stunning. I'd caught Tate admiring her a few times.

Della and I lived in the home Jimmy had bought for himself and me, only we spent all our time down my end of the house. She hadn't gone to see her parents yet, and I often asked what was holding her back. Only she wouldn't say, and I didn't want to pester her. Not when she was smiling more each day. The smallest of noises could scare her and if a male got too close, she would cringe away. She still had a fair way to go to get back to the determined, fierce, and confident woman she'd been when I'd met her.

While I went to work, she stayed in the house and watched movies or read.

I could understand her need to want a vacation and relax after everything, but I worried it would drag out her road to recovery.

Handle still hadn't left. He said he would at the end of the month. At least then they'd be certain no fallback would come to bite us on the butt. He stayed with Della at the house every day, and I was sure being in one place each and every day was starting to get to him. He was moodier than the first day I'd met him.

The police had finally put the whole scene at the house down to unsolved. They couldn't confirm anything due to a lack of evidence. However, they eventually found out what a bad man Jimmy was after an anonymous email was sent to the lead detective with everything I had on Jimmy and what he'd done to young women—the kidnapping and raping. There wasn't much evidence, but it was enough for them to know he was a piece of shit. I think, due to the fact they never knew what Jimmy had been capable of, they were quicker to place his case unsolved. I also had sent what I'd found on the detective who'd taken me to Jimmy. He was in debt up to his eyeballs, which was how Jimmy had him on his payroll.

Of course, when they'd told me who my husband really was, I broke down in front of them.

Having my name cleared from the case eased fear from my heart, and it also meant I could go to Dallas sooner. Though, we still didn't want to risk moving suspicion to the Hawks, which could happen if I got on a flight and left town to move so I could get to know my boyfriend.

Boyfriend.

It was a funny word for Dallas. He certainly wasn't a boy and we hadn't started as friends.

Yet, he meant a lot to me.

Even that seemed crazy. A man I was still getting to know meant something to me already.

"Tiny?" he called through the phone, dragging me from my thoughts.

"Yeah, Viking man?"

"I asked if you thought of mentionin' to Della to move here with you?"

My brows dipped, unsure. "I'll see how things go once she sees her parents. I don't know why she's holding back." I sighed. "Anyway, are you asking for her sake or mine... or Handle's?"

He snorted. "All of the above, darlin'."

"I knew Handle had a thing for her. I see him watching her—"

"Tiny, don't go there, okay? My brother has his own shit to deal with. I ain't sure if he'll be good for her or her for him."

"Yeah, I can see something's on his mind and has been for a long time."

"Never thought I'd get all mushy and shit, but I wish you were comin' sooner my way."

Laughing, I cooed, "Aw, you can be sweet."

"Woman," he growled low through the phone.

"Oh, did I tell you I decided I'm moving in with Julian?"

"The fuck?" he snarled. "I ain't havin' you in Ballarat when I'm in Melbourne—" He broke off when he heard my laugh. "Stop messin' with me when I can't punish you for it in person."

"I can't help it. It's like it brings joy to my life. Anyway, I did decide to take you up on your offer to find me a house. But, like I said, as long as you get Julian's help to pick."

He groaned. "Darlin', I can pick a house you'll like without him."

"Dallas, humour me, okay? You're a manly man. I need a house that will be me—"

"I know you," he clipped.

"You're getting there, yes—"

"And I can send you the goddamn links to the houses. I do not need to have Julian come and look at each one with me."

He acted like I was asking him to pull all his teeth from his mouth. I grinned at how uncomfortable a gay man made my Viking man. Still, I explained, "I'd like you two to spend time with each other. He's my friend, Dallas, which means he'll be around a lot. From the links you give me on the houses, I'll narrow it down. But I'd like you both to see the places in person. *Please.*"

"Fuck," he huffed. "The things you make me do, woman. Is this what being in a… in a r-relationship means? If so, you'll owe me huge for it."

Lying back on the bed, I burst out laughing. He cracked me up every time he choked over the word relationship. After calming down, I smiled, hearing his grumbling on the other end of the line. I knew he'd never been in a relationship before. He honestly never thought much of women, but it warmed me all over he wanted to try for me.

"Dallas, I'll do just about anything for you if you do this for me."

"Anything?" he asked, and I just knew his brow would have risen and wicked thoughts would be running through his mind. My Viking man liked a bit of kink—tying up, choking, spanking —so it was lucky he was the only man I'd let try those things on me. Just the thought of doing them with him turned me on.

He could punish me and order me in the bedroom all he liked, which I told him just the previous day. But it had to end as soon as we stepped out the door.

"Anything," I purred, then added, "Within reason, of course."

He snorted. "Yeah, Tiny, within reason."

"Okay, let's move on to something we don't know about each other." I had been asking him this question each time we called one another. I wanted to know everything there was about Dallas Gan. We'd started with favourite things, family, and dislikes. The question I was going to ask should have been one I asked at the start, which I realised earlier that day when I thought of it. "When's your birthday?"

All I got was air on the other end.

"Dallas?"

"Shit. I don't want anything."

"Viking man, *when* is it?"

He grunted. "Coming up."

"Dal—" There was a knock at my bedroom door. "Hang on one second," I told Dallas, and before he could bitch about it, I pulled the phone away from my ear. "Come in," I called.

Della opened the door enough to pop her head in. "Hey, um, can we talk for a second?"

"Sure. I'll just say bye to Dallas, one sec."

As soon as I had my phone up, Dallas said before he ended the call, "Call you later, Tiny. Go see to your girl."

My whole body sighed, if that was possible, at how incredible he was. Then again, he was getting out of talking about his birthday, which was coming up. I just had no idea how soon that was. I'd have to do some investigating later if I wanted to give him a gift. Only what would a man like Dallas want?

"Sorry." I smiled at Della and shook my head, putting the phone to the bed. "Come on in and sit." I patted the spot next to me. She came in and sat, her eyes to her lap where she absently played with the hem of her tee. "What's happening?"

"I was hoping that tomorrow you could take it off from work and we could, um, go get our hair done and stuff.... Then I'd like to go see my parents in the afternoon."

"Really?"

"Yes. I've put things off enough. I need to move past it all, and that means seeing them. The thing is they, look, they're not the same as they used to be. Losing Ashley hit them hard and then with me, when I wouldn't listen and stay out of it all, it was hard for them. They don't know where I've been. They think I ran off to deal with Ashley's death on my own. They thought I stayed out of it all, when I didn't. I'm not sure how they'll be, but I need to tell them everything."

She had asked me to leave the video I'd had on Ashley with Jimmy out of what I sent to the detective who had been on the case. She'd been the one who wanted to tell her parents what we'd found and not the police. I did as asked. It wasn't my sister. I could only hope they understood why vengeance had burned inside of Della to take Jimmy down and why, in the end, it blew up in her face, causing her to live her own personal nightmare.

Her sister had meant everything to her.

I would have done the same, even if my mum had asked me to stay well away from it all.

"I think they'll just be happy to see you," I said gently.

She shrugged. "We'll see." Looking up, she asked again, "Will you come with me, haircut and then parents?"

After rolling my eyes, I winked and replied, "Of course I will. No matter what, Del, you and me, we stick together."

"Yeah." She smiled. "I'll go tell Handle what our plans are."

"You know he'll come, right?"

She nodded, her jaw clenching. "I know."

"What will we tell your parents about him? Can't say he's your boyfriend."

"Maybe he can be your security detail for the day?"

"Yes, that could work. After all, Jimmy's death and my taking over the company and appointing Tate as CEO has been all over the news." I'd had many calls in the first two weeks with people wanting interviews. I declined each and every one, stating I just wanted to get on with my life. Most had left it, thought there were a few pesky ones still hounding me. Another reason I couldn't up and leave for Melbourne. I was hoping they would all go away after they found out about Jimmy's double life. Then again, it could draw more attention my way once more.

Fuck.

I hadn't thought of that.

After Della had left, I put all depressing thoughts out of my mind and picked up my phone again. I pressed in the stored number and waited.

"Hello, my cheese to my mac," came cheerily from the other end.

"Hi, Julian. Are you over your little snit?"

He huffed. "If you mean by keeping all your juicy information about what Dallas Gan is like in bed, then no. However, you may redeem yourself once you are living closer to me by buying me chocolates, flowers, and candy every day for the rest of your life."

The morning after Dallas had left, I got a phone call from Julian ripping me a new one with how worried he'd been for me. He said he'd felt like a shit losing contact with me in the first place, but even more so when he knew he could have helped me if we'd still been close. We argued over the fact it was both of our faults we'd lost contact once again; the first time was when I'd been in Ballarat. We'd yelled over the fact we were both stubborn when I didn't reach out for his help, like he hadn't when he had his situation with his parents. Eventually, we forgave each other and promised to tell one another everything from then on. Of course, it didn't last long when I refused to tell him every detail of Dallas's body and how he pleased me in bed.

"Will it help that I've asked Dallas to take you with him to see the houses I'm thinking of buying?"

"Hmm. Okay. Actually, oh my God, yes! A full day of torturing… I mean getting to know my bestie's man is perfect."

"Go easy on him, please. I do want you two to get along enough you won't get banned when he's around."

"Fine," he sighed, and knowing Julian, he would have said it with an eye-roll.

"I also need to ask a favour."

"What's that, my icing to my cake?"

"Dallas's birthday is coming up, and he won't tell me what date. I don't even know how old he is or what to get him."

"You don't know how old he is? The man you're dating?"

"Shut up, we're still getting to know one another."

"Maybe I should be the one dating him, at least I know how old he's turning…. Kidding, poppet. You're man enough for me." I burst out laughing. Mattie must have caught him talking shit once again. "Anyway. He's turning the big four-o."

"Forty?" I breathed.

"Yes."

"Butternut, it's only nine years difference between the two of you. Don't stress."

"Oh, no. I won't. I was just surprised. He looks good for his age."

"That he does. Not as good as my Mattie though, love you, poppet." I heard him blow a kiss to his man.

"Julian?"

"Yes? Oh, I have to go. My man just gave me 'the look.'"

"Julian!" I snapped.

"What? I love you, I do, but I'm not missing out on any action for you."

"Jesus." I sighed. "Can you please just find out when his birthday is and an idea of what to get him?"

"Of course, and I already know what you can get him."

"What?" I asked.

"You."

CHAPTER TEN

DALLAS

A bullet to the brain would have been more fun than what I was dealing with. I was standing in the third house we'd looked at for Tiny with Julian next to me oohing and ahhing all over the goddamn place. I rubbed at my temples again. My head was killing me.

"This place is it. I have that feeling, He-Man."

"You said that about the last one," I gritted.

"Yes, but that one didn't have the open fireplace. I know my girl has always wanted one of those and the wall colouring... what is that?" he asked the realtor, only he didn't give the woman a chance to reply. "Doesn't matter what it is actually, it's divine. OMG, look, Luke Cage, this kitchen is bigger, and it has a walk-in pantry." He stepped inside and I contemplated locking him in there and leaving him to rot. Then again, Tiny would have my arse if she decided it was this house she wanted and found her friend dead in there.

So I let him go on and on about whatever the fuck he was, I think it had something to do with the taps, and turned from the kitchen to go back into the living area. The room was big. I liked it being that way since I was a big guy myself. The place was the better one we'd seen and what made it even more so was the fact it was closer than the others to the compound. To me.

Could I see myself living in that house?

Sure.

Only I knew it wouldn't happen for a while. I'd let Tiny move into it and visit—every fucking night—then eventually she'd find out I'd slowly moved all I owned in. I didn't have a place of my own. I had a heap of money saved, but I never wanted a place to call my own. I liked living in the compound. My brothers were there. The club sluts were there when I needed to wet my dick, and my work was right there. Everything I needed.

Until Tiny.

Now all I could imagine was having our own place, going from work to a house my woman would be in.

Fuck. That shit freaked me the hell out. I was starting to sweat. I wasn't a one-woman man. I didn't see the point to getting to know a woman when all I needed from them was a tight hole to place my cock and get off.

However, Tiny was more.

So much more I couldn't even put it down to one thing about her. It was all of her I wanted to keep in my life. I wanted to see every day.

Scary as fuck.

Especially when I knew that feeling late at night—or even when my mind wandered to what she was doing—was me missing her.

I couldn't understand how she made such an impact on me to where I was now dating her, but she had and…. Christ, I knew why my brothers settled for the one.

I wasn't saying she was going to be it, but everything was pointing that way.

My brothers were as shocked at me as I was with myself. The club sluts more so when they tried shit with me, and I told them to fuck off, I had a woman.

Bloody hell.

I had a woman.

One of my own.

Did that mean she'd put out for me whenever I wanted?

I palmed my forehead at the thought of her denying me between her legs. If that shit happened, I didn't know how I'd feel about it.

Still, I'd learn.

I was fucking learning already.

Shit, I was suddenly a giver also. Explained why I was stuck with the gay dude for the day looking at houses.

As I walked down the hall, I took in the structure, tapping the hell out of the wall. It was good. Wouldn't fall and crush her small body. A pain slashed through my chest. Crap, was that fear for my woman? I had to check the electricity; the wiring could be faulty and shock her to death. Hell, and the gas. I didn't want her falling asleep one night not to wake up the next because of a gas leak.

Motherfucker. How did my brothers put up with the worry for their women?

Idiots, the lot of them, yet I was now one as well.

Would I want it another way?

Would I want to tell Tiny to fuck off and never see her again?

Damn, the thought of not hearing her, seeing her, and feeling her in any way was a panic attack waiting to happen. I rubbed at my chest.

Yeah. She was it, and I was a goddamn pansy.

Sighing, I looked at the ceiling. The fan on the roof seemed uneven. I'd want that checked in case it suddenly fell and cut off her head.

Groaning, I looked to the floor. I was going to have to gut the place if she bought it and redo everything myself. At least then I'd know it'd be safe.

"Hey, big man, what you doing in here? Oh, wow. She will love that window seat." Julian rushed in and over to sit on the window seat and gazed out at the garden.

"If she buys it, I'm doing all the renovations. I don't trust those builder fuckers for rippin' her off and doin' it a dodge way to get it done faster."

"I'm sure she won't—"

"There're so many things that could go wrong. If they didn't take care and let something slip by and she was harmed by it... I'd have to kill them. I don't mind killin' people, but—"

"Hey," Julian snapped and came to stand beside me. "Keep the talk about killing to a minimum, or like... at all. The realtor could hear you."

Clenching my jaw, I clipped, "This is serious shit, Julian. If this is the house for her, I want everything checked. The gas, electricity, a pest inspection. I want to know if the house is weak and would likely fall on her head when she sleeps. She won't know. She'll be sound asleep and... fuck."

My heart was rapid in my chest from all the crazy thoughts.

I knew I was being pathetic, but Tiny was worth the risk I was taking by claiming her as mine. I didn't want anything to happen to her.

"It's fine. You're fine and she'll be fine. We'll make sure of it," he reassured me and slowly rubbed my back.

"I'm being—"

"Don't. You're being you. A man who's gruff and huffs, puffs—"

"I swear if you tell me I'll blow a house down, I'll fuckin' punch you."

He chuckled. "Aw, you know *Three Little Pigs*, that's awesome. I was reading that to—"

"Julian," I barked low.

He sighed. "Well, I wasn't going to say that. You're a man's man, so you're not in tune with your feelings. Our Melissa brings them out in you, and you're still trying to deal with that. Just go with it, and you shouldn't care what anyone thinks. Except the killing talk can be cut right out."

Never thought I'd see the day when I'd be getting advice from a gay guy.

"I think Tiny will like this place," I said, suddenly feeling awkward. I stepped forward and his hand dropped away.

"It's okay, big man, we'll keep this bonding moment to ourselves. At least I know now you won't kick me out when I visit, right?"

"Until you get on my nerves."

"Ha!" he yelled and pointed at me. "You just admitted you see yourself here also with Melissa." I rolled my eyes at him. He went on, "And yes, I can see our girl liking this place the most. Oh, by the way, you may need this back." He pulled out my wallet from the back pocket of his jeans, opened it and grabbed my ID out. Storming forward, I snatched both off him. He looked up smiling. "Now I can tell Melissa when your birthday is."

"Fuck."

"I may be gay, Dallas, but I can be cunning."

"Let's get outta here. We givin' the last one a miss?"

"Yeah," he agreed and skipped to the door. "At least then we can continue on with our guys' night. Up next on our bonding trip is booze. I would say boobs and boinking, but I'm not one for boobs, and I think our partners would be upset if we boinked." He winked and left the room after I gave him the finger. Then I cringed and gagged at the sudden thought of Julian naked.

Fucking prick mentioning boinking when I was already supporting a semi most of the time from thinking of my woman was just too damn much.

I suppose the guy was okay. That was if he didn't talk, and after spending time with him, I only wanted to run or punch his lights out a few times instead of all the time.

That said something, right?

At least that was what I'd tell Melissa.

Leaving the bedroom, I took one last look around. Yeah, I could see the bed by the wall beside the bathroom. Some drawers on each side of the bed. A dog laying on a rug I'd buy for the house at the end of the bed. Not some pansy-arse little dog. I was talking a big boxer dog. One that could add extra protection for my woman.

At least Julian and I were on the same page about the house. Since I could picture Melissa already flittering around the place doing whatever women did, I wanted that image to come true. I wanted to see her cooking, cleaning, and on her laptop while I did my own shit around the place.

Well, look the fuck at me.

I was thinking domesticated thoughts.

Did I need to shoot myself now or go with the flow?

To hell with it. If it kept Tiny at my side, I'd go for it.

Entering the living room, I stopped still. My eyes widened and my fists clenched along with my jaw. All that reaction because the realtor was now sobbing onto Julian's shoulder.

"What in the fuck happened?" I swear if he screwed anything up for Melissa and the house, I wouldn't care my woman loved the guy. I'd gut him.

"She's having a hard time right now with her boyfriend. Men

are such arseholes sometimes. There, there. Let it out, honey." He patted her back and cooed down at her in a mumbled tone.

Run.

It was all I wanted to do.

Not only was I in a goddamn house with a gay guy I could only stand for short spurts of time, but there was also a crying woman.

"This gonna take long?" I asked and got a glare from both of them.

Swear to Christ, Melissa had better appreciate the shit I put up with for her.

My stomach grumbled, telling me missing out on lunch wasn't a good idea. I glanced at my phone to check the time. "Can we wrap the tears up? I'm starved."

"Dallas Gan, stop being a douche," Julian clipped at me, throwing me another glare.

Fucking hell.

"See what my bestie will have to put up with? He must be good in bed if she's moving here for him. Anyway, I bet your man didn't mean to say what he did. Why don't I ring him for you and find out?"

Jesus.

"I've been good. *Real* good, but I swear, Julian, if you don't get your arse in the car and let the woman deal with her own problem, you will find my fist shoved down your throat."

"Oh, all right," he snapped and gave one last long-arse hug to the realtor before telling her, "You'll be okay." He patted her arm and made his way to the front door where I was standing. Over his shoulder, he added, "Oh, and we'll call you about the house. Later."

Please, God, Satan, whoever the fuck will listen, give me strength to not kill the man.

CHAPTER ELEVEN

MELISSA

*D*ella and I felt so much better having our hair and nails done. Still, I could see the fear in her eyes as we drove our way to her parents' house. I kept looking to the back seat giving her, what I hoped, a reassuring smile as she fidgeted with her seat belt, her hands, and her clothes. Handle was driving. Of course he'd come with us, as well as for our beauty treatments. He'd sat and read all the magazines while the women who worked there checked him out all morning long. He never said much, and from the glares he shot everyone, I guessed he hated the attention as well.

"We're here," Handle said gruffly. He pulled to a stop out the front of a small weatherboard home and then stopped the car. He didn't move, neither did Della. Glancing around, I saw her just staring out the window at her old home.

"You ready?"

"No," she whispered, but opened the door anyway. Handle

was out before I managed to exit. I went to Della's side and took her hand, wondering why she was so hesitant to see her parents. I knew she'd said they'd be upset for her to continue her investigation on Jimmy, but wouldn't they also be relieved to see her and know she was okay?

Her hand shook in mine. With her free one, she straightened out her dress and walked up the steps to the front door. When she just stood there, Handle leaned around and knocked on the front door, causing Della to jump.

We waited in silence. At first I thought no one was home and wondered if they worked. Then I heard loud, pounding footsteps approach. The door swung open and in it stood a man in his late fifties wearing sweatpants and a tee.

His eyes widened a fraction and then narrowed as he took us all in. Finally, they stayed on his daughter. "What did you do?" he demanded.

I stiffened and gripped Della's hand harder. There was no warm welcome, nothing to say how much he'd missed her.

"Mr Kent, I'm—"

"I know who you are. You were married to that bastard and she brought you here." He sneered down at me. "Who's he?"

Straightening, I jutted my chin up and said, "He works for me."

"Honey, who is it?" was called and then a woman, just as old as her husband, appeared down the end of the hall. Her hand fluttered to her neck. "Mardella."

"Hi, Mum," Della whispered.

"Can we come in?" Handle asked.

Mr Kent stepped back. We walked in and down the hall towards Mrs Kent. She shuffled back and turned, and we followed her into a living room. Mrs Kent fell into one couch, Della and I sat opposite with Handle standing behind us. Once Mr Kent came in, he sat next to his wife, glaring at us.

"I…." Della started then stopped to take a deep breath. "Do you know where I've been?" she asked.

Mr Kent snorted. "Off having a good time."

"No." She shook her head. "I know you both wished for me to leave Ashley's murder to the police, but I couldn't."

Mrs Kent gasped. Mr Kent snapped, "What the hell? Is this how you got close to that prick's wife?"

"No, Melissa helped me. She—"

"I don't give a fuck about her. What did you do?"

My eyes widened at him. Shock was the only word I could use to describe my reaction to Mr Kent's tone to his own daughter. Fuck, they hadn't even hugged her, let alone greeted her with a hello.

"I couldn't let him off. We knew he was the one to take Ashley. We knew. So I did some digging myself. I got a job within one of his businesses, only I wasn't getting enough on him, which was how Melissa came into it. She was helping me, but we both got caught." Mrs Kent cried out. "I'm okay, now, Mum."

"What did they do?" Mr Kent asked.

"It doesn't matter what they did. It's over now. Jimmy had been the one to take Ashley and… he did murder her."

Mrs Kent started crying. At least Mr Kent showed enough emotion to wrap his wife up and hold her close.

"It's over, Mum. He's dead. I'm sure you've seen it on the news."

"Get out," Mr Kent ordered.

"Joe!" Mrs Kent yelled.

Shaking his head, he said, "We don't need you here, making us relive what we went through losing Ashley. You never listened to us. You didn't care—"

"I did, he's dead. We can breathe easier knowing Ashley's murderer is gone."

"You went after him, not caring how we would react when you didn't come back to us. It's been three months, Mardella. Three months. We didn't know if you were alive or dead. So don't say you cared. You didn't. You only worried about yourself and look at what's happened to you. You're not the person you used to be—"

"I lost my sister and no one was doing anything about it," Della screamed.

Mr Kent stood and yelled back, "And we lost both our daughters the day we lost Ashley. You should have stayed away—"

"Joe, please," Mrs Kent wailed, reaching her hand out to her husband's arm.

Handle walked around the couch, took hold of Della's arm and made her stand. My heart was beating a million miles an hour. I couldn't... I didn't know what or how to think. I was shocked by the way her father was treating her.

"We're leavin'," Handle stated.

"Good." Mr Kent nodded. "Should never have adopted you. You brought us more pain after losing our only child."

"Don't," Della begged.

"Enough," Handle snarled. "Not one more fuckin' word outta you. This woman standing before you did what most people wouldn't. She fought for her sister when no one else was. She went through hell to do it, and you say this crap to her after it all?" He shook his head, sneering at them. "You're both pathetic and don't deserve her in your lives." Before anyone could say a word, he led a silent, crying Della from the room.

Standing, I sighed and tried to get my thoughts together, but my emotions were riding high. "I hope you regret what you've said to her. She's a brave, strong woman, and the pain she was put through by Jimmy and his men was worse than anything you could think of. Yet, I think the pain you've just inflicted on her was worse because it came from people who took her in, who cared for her, showed her love and now, now you've as good as ripped out her heart." Keeping Mr Kent's eyes, I added with disgust in my voice, "You should be ashamed of yourself."

A good fist to the eye would have been satisfying. Instead, I walked from the room. I heard Mrs Kent break down once more. I felt for her, but she didn't do anything to stop her husband crushing my friend. So I quickly dropped my sorrow for that woman. I hadn't known they were her adoptive parents, not that it mattered, and really it shouldn't have mattered to them either. I couldn't believe he'd thrown it back in Della's face like that. I clenched my teeth together from the anger I felt on her behalf.

Maybe it was his fear talking, saying those vile words to Della, but whatever it was, she didn't deserve that.

No one did.

Especially not after what she'd been through.

As I made my way to the car, I saw Handle standing on the outside leaning against the back door. When I grew closer, he bent in and said, "She's been hurt too much. She comes home with you when you do. You're the only one left for her. Don't make her lose you as well."

"I won't," I told him with certainty in my voice.

He grunted. "Good." He made his way around the car and got in the driver seat. I didn't bother getting into the front. I slipped into the back and expected to find Della in tears. It worried me when all she did was stare out the window.

Handle started the car and drove off. I took Della's hand, only she pulled from my grasp and placed both hands on her lap. Her eyes still out the window.

"Della, honey," I tried.

She said nothing. I chanced a glance to Handle up front, and he caught my gaze. Concern filled his hard eyes and dipping brows.

I laid a hand on her arm. "Della, please."

She turned her head to me. I clenched my teeth and willed my tears not to fall. My belly dropped to the pit of my stomach.

Her eyes were dead.

There was nothing inside of them.

No hurt.

No pain.

Nothing.

And that scared me.

"Honey, *please*, please don't listen to him. Don't fear his words. He wouldn't have meant—"

"He did," she said in an emotionless tone that wasn't hers. "I always saw it growing up. I wasn't their child. It doesn't matter. I would have done the same for Ashley, regardless of how they feel. She was my sister even if we weren't born by the same parents." She shook her head and shrugged. "I don't care. I no longer care about anything." Her gaze went back out the window, trying to shut me out also.

"Well, I do care. I care about you. You have me, Della. I know it's not the same, but I need you to know I'll always be there for you. I'll—"

"Please. Just… drop it. For now, I just want to sit here."

Oh fuck. I'd lost her.

Tears pooled. I hated, despised him, all of them, every single soul who'd done Della wrong and made her feel this way.

Gently, I rubbed her arm and then let my hand drop to the seat. I wiped at my face with my other hand and sucked a deep shuddering breath in through my nose.

My friend wasn't there anymore.

But I would do everything I could to bring her back.

Shit.

Fucking hell.

I hoped I could.

No, I would.

One way or another, I would bring the confident Della back. If she fought, I would fight back just as hard. If she ran, I would follow. Looking in the mirror, I knew I wouldn't be the only one helping her either. It may take time, a new destination, and some more friends. But we would get there.

We had to.

Handle was right: She'd lost too much. And now it was time to gain everything and a lot more back.

CHAPTER TWELVE

MELISSA

A week passed and Della was still the same. She hardly spoke. She never smiled or laughed. The night after we'd arrived back from her parents', I even tried to gain a reaction from her when I showed her the texts I received from Dallas about his trip with Julian to see the houses. All I got was a nod.

I wanted to know what was going through her mind. I wanted her to open up to me, but she didn't, or wouldn't, couldn't. Each and every night as the week passed, I tried to talk to her, and each and every time she replied with, "Not now."

Worry for her consumed me. Dallas could even hear it when we talked. I was surprised when he suggested for her to speak with a professional. I thought it a good idea, only I didn't know how I was going to suggest it to Della.

In the end, I didn't.

When I spoke to Handle about it, he suggested getting someone to see her without telling her beforehand.

After a few calls, I found a woman by the name of Elina Panton. She sounded lovely and kind on the phone. I asked if she made home visits since Della was back to not leaving the house. She did. So I organised her to arrive Friday night.

Once I had Elina in the kitchen, I went to Della's room and asked her to come help me with dinner. She opened her door and followed me to the kitchen silently, only to come to an abrupt halt.

"Della, this is Elina. She's here to have a chat with you. I thought maybe it would be good if you spoke to someone you didn't know." I bit my bottom lip with hope in my heart she didn't tell me to fuck off and run from the room. Then again, with Handle standing behind her, she wouldn't have had much luck.

"Hi, Della. Honestly, I'm here to have a cup of coffee with you and if you want to talk you can. If you don't, that's fine."

I watched as Della's whole body stiffened. My mouth opened ready to say something, but then she said, "Coffee."

Elina smiled and nodded. "Yes."

When Della nodded in reply, my whole body sagged in relief. She was going to try. That was all I wanted. "Um, I have to go and make a phone call. The coffee's in the pot ready to be poured." I exited the room with a warm touch to Della's hand. Handle had already disappeared somewhere, so I made my way to my bedroom. For a while, I paced the room and prayed Della would be okay with what I had organised. I also prayed Elina would get Della to talk and, by doing so, it could help Della.

I hadn't lied when I said I'd be making a phone call, so to keep my mind off what was going on in the kitchen, I grabbed my phone and pressed in the saved number.

"Hello, my cake to my cream. To what do I owe the honour of receiving your call?"

Julian had phoned me the day after his bonding time with

Dallas. He told me how much he enjoyed giving him shit. He also mentioned how he felt Dallas was good for me. The house they'd suggested, I'd decided to go with. Of course Dallas said he'd have all the renovations done by the time I relocated, and I had to laugh when Julian tried to tell me he wouldn't be surprised if the house was childproof either. Apparently, Dallas had an overprotective streak for me. Though Julian could have been exaggerating. He did tend to do that.

The main detail I asked for was to have Julian find out his date of birth, which he did. I had a month to come up with a perfect present.

However, a thought had flown into my mind earlier, and I wanted to check with Julian to see if it would be possible.

"Hey, my BFF."

"You need something. What is it?"

"How did you know?" I asked.

"You only pull out the BFF when you really want something."

Rolling my eyes, I smiled and admitted, "Fine. You're right, I do want something."

"Enlighten me, my pretty."

"Well, with Dallas's birthday coming up, I kept thinking about what you said, how all he'd want for a present would be me. I'm going to give it to him."

"Oookay, as in what way? Your virgin arse?"

I gasped, "Julian!" then laughed. I loved talking with him; he always shocked me, made me laugh and smile. "No. I mean I'm going to fly in."

"Oh, yay. When? Do you want me to come get you at the airport?"

"Yes, please. I'll have Della with me, and I'm sure Handle will want to come back to stay home. However, I also need something else. You know how you've got a spare room."

"Spit it out, girlfriend."

"Okay. I somehow need you to get Dallas to Ballarat to your home so in case anyone, cops, reporters or anything like that is still watching me, it will look like I'm visiting you and your friend just shows up. Only you, Mattie, and my gorgeous dumpling, Aeila, can't be home."

"Are you telling me you want to boink your boyfriend in our spare room?"

"Um, yes."

"Okay, just checking. I'm all down to help a sister out by her getting a bit. Now, leave all the planning to me. You just show up on his birthday. Ooh, I'll drag some of the boys into it, get them to organise a ride down our way and somehow get him to my place where you'll be waiting. Then I'll sneak out without anyone seeing me. I could wear a disguise or something. I feel like I'm a superhero."

Laughter burst out of me. My friend was crazy awesome. I knew getting Julian to help would be a good decision. "You are my hero if you can pull all of this off."

"Oh, I will, be sure of that. Now, I must be off to start planning. We'll talk soon."

"We will, thanks, J-man."

"Anything for you. Ciao."

Hanging up, I thought of sneaking down the hall to see how things were going for Della. I hoped she hadn't just kicked Elina out after Handle and I had left the room.

I hadn't yet told Della about our trip to Victoria or the fact I was going to plead with her to move with me when the time came. Nothing in Sydney was holding her back. Maybe a change of scenery would help. I didn't know, but I did wish it that way.

My belly dipped in excitement thinking of moving. I couldn't wait to get out of Sydney since I knew there was also nothing that held me there, and Tate was more than a CEO. He ran all the businesses well, something I could never have done.

94
94
94

My phone dinged with a message. Glancing down, I smiled.

Mum: **How's my dove?**

Me: **Good. Missing her mum though.**

Mum: **Well, get your tush to QLD.**

Reading the message again, I rubbed my thumb over it. The day after Jimmy had died, I'd called my mum to let her know I was alive. She knew nothing of Jimmy, not until she saw a picture of me on the news. Of course, that phone call didn't go down well. I ended up coming clean about the whole situation. She cried and yelled, while I bawled. In the end, she understood I wanted to help Della out. It was amazing to be in contact all the time with her once again. She knew nothing about the Hawks man, from their charter in Queensland, watching her under Dodge's orders in case what Jimmy had said was true.

Me: **Soon I will and I'd like to bring someone with me.**

Mum: **WHO????**

Me: **Someone I met through the Jimmy situation. He helped me, Mum. He protected me.**

Mum: **I would love to meet him then. What's his name?**

Me: **Dallas.**

Mum: **Nice strong name. Are you happy?**

She always asked me this in every phone call or text.

Me: **Yes. Very!**

Mum: **Then I'm happy. But I have to go. I'm heading to the movies with some friends.**

Me: **Love you, Mum.**

Mum: **Love you, my dove, always.**

Even though I still worried for Della, my heart was warm and full for the first time in a long time. Not only have I let my mum know my life was better than it had ever been, but it was also because of the relationship I had with a certain man. Who would have thought through phone calls and messages I would get to know who Dallas

Gan was and like him more each day? Of course he had his days where he was an arse. I would also have mine where I was a bitch, but it was what we had in between that counted.

Was one month enough to just about love someone?

I wasn't sure, but I knew my feelings for Dallas were strong.

As I pressed in his number, I placed the phone against my ear and smiled. If he wasn't busy, I knew he'd take my mind off Della in the kitchen. I wouldn't venture out there until I knew for sure Elina was gone, and as I walked over to my window, I saw her car still in the drive. I sighed in relief, just as a gruff voice answered with, "Tiny."

"Hey, Viking man. What are you up to?"

"Just sittin' in the compound at the bar. What you doin'?"

"Just waiting on Della to finish talking with Elina."

"Darlin', you got someone?"

"Yeah, thank you for suggesting it. I think, no, I hope it will help her."

"Fuck, I do too. Hate seein' you worry."

"You can be sweet, you know."

"From the looks my brothers are givin' me, they're thinkin' that, which means I'm gonna have to beat one of them."

I threw my head back and laughed. "So who's with you there?"

"Pick, Billy, Dodge, Dive, and a few others."

"Women?"

"Maybe."

Irritation stirred in me. He'd told me a few club women had tried shit with him, but he said he was with someone. "Dallas," I bit out.

His chuckle was sweet to hear, but it annoyed me right then. "My woman jealous?"

"Fuck yes. I'm not there to give you what you want."

"Relax, Tiny. They're over the other side of the room while Low, Mena, and Josie are havin' some make-up shit party."

"Okay, well, good."

"Enjoy hearin' you get riled though."

"Be better if I was there so you could screw it out of me."

"Woman," he growled in the back of his throat. "Now's not the time to get cute with me. Fuck, they're givin' me looks. I—" A loud crash came through the phone. "The fuck?" Dallas clipped. "Shit, gotta go, Tiny, talk soon."

"Everything okay?"

"Yeah, darlin', but whoever's pissed Beast off may not be. We're gonna see if we can calm him."

"Take care."

"You too," he said and then hung up. Beast was a silent, mountain of a biker, as big as Dallas. He was also sweet and I was sure shy. I hoped he was okay.

It was sometime later, while I was watching *Vikings* on Netflix, there was a hesitant knock on my door. Sitting up, I called, "Come in."

When it came open, Della stood there. I couldn't read her expression before she said, "I've made some soup, would you like some?"

With a small smile, I nodded and stood. Following her down the hall, I stepped into the kitchen to see Handle already sitting at the table and no Elina.

I took a seat at the table as Della brought over two bowls. "It's nothing special, but I thought you both may be hungry."

Handle grunted. Rolling my eyes at him, I grinned up at Della and said, "Thanks, smells great."

She grabbed her own bowl and sat at the end of the table. Handle was on one side of her and me on the other. I picked up my spoon and dug in. I hadn't realised just how hungry I was. The room felt awkward. I wanted to know, as I was sure Handle did also, how things went with Elina or if we stepped too far by organising it. However, I kept quiet and ate my soup.

It was obvious Handle had other ideas when he said, "You shitty with us organising Elina here?" I was surprised he added himself in there. Maybe he didn't want me to take the full fallout if it hadn't been the best idea, which I found sweet.

Della placed her spoon in the bowl and templed her fingers under her chin, elbows resting on the table. "At first, I hated you both, and Elina."

Shit.

"But then"—I sat straighter and placed my own spoon down, ready to hear more—"I found Elina easy to talk to." She shrugged, and it was then I noticed her eyes were more alive. My body gave off a jolt of optimism. Della placed her hands down to her lap and looked at her bowl. "To start with, we talked about random things. Well, she did. I sat there drinking my coffee and fuming over the whole situation you both put me in."

Double shit.

She looked up to us. "Until she told me about something she'd been through. I was shocked because she seemed so put together." She smiled for the first time in a week. "Thank you. Both of you. I-I still have a way to go, but what you did for me, bringing Elina here, it helped." Her next words were on a whisper. "It doesn't hurt so much to breathe, to live anymore."

Which told me she was still in pain, but to know it had eased inside of her, even a little bit, brought tears to my eyes. It also meant, with Elina's help, she could find herself once again.

EPILOGUE

DALLAS

*I*t'd been two months since I'd seen my woman and it was hitting me hard. Maybe my brothers could sense it, which was why I was on my Harley riding from Melbourne to Ballarat to visit with the other brothers. I also reckon it had some crap to do with my birthday, but I wasn't up for a goddamn party. If they did something stupid like a surprise party, the mood I was in, I could pull my gun and shoot the lot of them. I was also pissed because I'd tried calling Tiny earlier but she wasn't answering. Of course my mind played games with me and placed her in all scenarios like she was abducted by aliens because she would have fuckin' called or told Tate where she fucking was. When I rang Tate, he said, "As far as I know she's at some spa thing with Della." Which explained why I couldn't reach Della either.

What was the damn spa place like on lockdown with no communication devices? Not that he'd known which goddamn spa it was. I didn't go as far as ringing all spa places around their area. I managed to hold off because I didn't want to seem like too much of a creeper. *Too* much.

At least the ride was good. Getting out with my brothers was what I needed, even though it gave me time to think more. The end result was that I needed to see my woman. I wanted to see her, feel her, and have her under me as I slid my cock inside of her.

Jesus, I hadn't jerked off so much in my bloody life.

Once a-fucking-gain, I was hard just thinking of her. Her sweet mouth, tiny body, attitude, and wet pussy.

I was crazy for her, and not being around her was sending me insane. I wished to Christ the reporters and shit would leave her the fuck alone so she could move already. Just the other day she said she'd give it another two months for things to die down. Two months could fucking kill me.

As we rode into Ballarat and pulled up to the first set of lights, Dodge beside me turned and said, "We just gotta head to Julian's for a sec. He needs a hand with something."

I groaned. Dodge chuckled. "Come on now, I thought you two were close now."

"Fuck off," I snarled.

He took off from the lights chuckling. It was obvious God or whoever, was going to shit on me on my birthday by having me go to Julian's house.

Then again, the dude wasn't too bad in small, very goddamn small doses. I'd just make sure the visit was quick.

Get in and out, then head back to the Ballarat compound to drink my pansy emotions of missing Tiny away.

MELISSA

"Wait, you want me to what?" Julian screeched. We were standing in the spare room and I'd just asked Julian if he could do one last favour for me. Mattie had already left with Aeila and Della. Julian was going to leave as soon as he let Dallas into the house.

"Can you tie me to the bed?" I asked again.

He ran a hand over his face. "Lemon drop, you know I love you, and I'm happy you're happy, but don't you think this is overstepping just a little?"

"Julian, you've seen me naked so many times. Shit, you used to wax my twat. So what's a little tying among friends?" His head dropped back, eyes to the ceiling. "Besides, you won't actually see me naked. I'll strip while you're out of the room and lay under the sheet. Then call you back in."

"Jesus, the things I do for friends. Remind me to throw those sheets out and maybe burn the bed later."

I laughed. "Seriously? Wasn't it you who used my old apartment to have sex with whoever that guy was because you didn't want him to know where you lived?"

"Oh yeah. I forgot about that one. Okay, get naked, under the sheet and call me in. What are we using to tie you?"

"I brought some ties. They're in my bag. I'll get them out and place them on the bed. Have I told you today you're the best friend anyone could have?"

"Not today, but it's true. I am." He sent me an air kiss and left the room.

I quickly checked my phone and found another missed call from Dallas. He was going to be pissed I'd avoided him all day, and on his birthday as well.

There was also a message from Tate. Seemed Dallas had rung him as well. I giggled and sent him back a thanks for keeping up with the lie. I wasn't surprised Dallas had called Tate. It'd happened another time too when I was at the movies with Della and shut my phone down. Dallas hated not being able to reach me. Della had smiled over the fact of how protective he was. She was slowly getting back to who she was. Actually, I was sure she was becoming more of the person she'd been before Ashley even disappeared. She still had her dark days, but she went out more with me. She did the food shopping and cooking, and when I asked if she'd move with me to Melbourne, she'd said yes. I could even say she was excited about the change.

"You naked yet?" Julian called through the door.

Placing my phone on the bedside table, I yelled back, "Nearly." I flung my tee to the ground, unhooked my bra and slid down my jeans and panties. I'd already shaved, waxed, and buffed over my body ready for the night with my man.

Giddiness swept over me and swirled my belly in anticipation of Dallas's arrival. My body chilled to the cool room temperature. However, I knew once Dallas arrived, I would be smouldering.

As I slipped under the sheet and lay back, I smiled to the ceiling.

Soon I would have my man surrounding me in every way I wanted.

DALLAS

Dodge was the only one who came with me to Julian's. We parked out the front while the others continued into the compound across the road. Why didn't he rope another brother in to help so I could be already drinking since it was my goddamn birthday? Then again, maybe I was right about a surprise party and not everyone had shown yet, or they were still putting together something. I swear to Christ, if they organised a stripper, I'd kick all their arses. I didn't need some fucked up half-naked woman trying to grind herself against me. There was only one woman for that, and she was in bloody Sydney having a spa day and apparently, it ran over until night.

Slipping from my Harley, I followed Dodge to the front door he was already knocking at. The door swung open to a grinning-like-a-fool Julian. "Well, hello there Dallas and Dodge," he yelled.

"Why in the fuck are you yellin'?" I glared.

His eyes flicked to Dodge, to me, to inside the house, then Dodge and me again. "You're older today. I didn't know if your hearing would be the same."

Sighing, I dropped my head. "Let's just fix whatever the fuck we have to and get the fuck out of here."

"Shit," Dodge said. "I forgot my toolkit. Be back in a sec, brother." He started down the path to his bike.

"Come on, come on. You're letting the cool night air in. Brrrr." He fake shivered and rubbed his arms. He shifted back so I could step in and closed the door behind him. "If you could just move the bed in the spare room to the other wall, which should leave enough room for the bookcase we're putting together."

"Can't this shit wait until tomorrow?" Fucking hell, I wanted to drink, shoot the shit, and relax.

"No," he yelped. "Um, well maybe, but I just need you to move the bed tonight at least."

"Fine," I clipped and made my way down the hall.

"It's the first one on the left," Julian called. "I'm just going to get a drink. Oh, by the way, happy birthday."

"Yeah, yeah," I grumbled as I opened the door and stepped in.

Then I froze solid. My heart tripped over a beat and then took off running.

"Fuck me," slipped past my lips.

"Happy birthday, Viking man." Tiny smiled from the bed.

"Fuck me," I repeated.

"Well, I would if…" She held up her hands, which were tied to the wooden bedhead. "…so you're going to have to do the fucking."

"Happy goddamn birthday to me."

She laughed, such a fucking fantastic sound, only I got to see it also. Watch her eyes close, her mouth open, her neck arch, and her chest rise and fall.

My woman was there.

Right in front of me.

And I was standing frozen like a tool.

"So this explains where you've been," I stated as I walked to the side of the bed and ran my eyes over her. The sheet hid her naked body, but it was thin enough to make out she didn't have clothes on. Her legs were spread. I looked at the bottom posts and saw more ties wrapped around them. My woman was tied down spread-eagle style for me.

My dick jerked behind my jeans.

"Who knows about this? Who helped?"

She shrugged. "Julian, Mattie, Della, and Dodge, I think. Why? Is this not okay?"

Shaking my head, I grinned. "Christ, I want everyone to know how fuckin' lucky I am to have the woman I've fallen for doing this for me. Offer herself up like the best present ever."

"Have you fallen?" she asked in a whispered tone.

"Fuck yes."

"Good." She smiled coyly up at me. "Because I've fallen too."

"Yeah?"

"Yes. Now can you unwrap your present already."

"Gladly." In seconds I had my tee off and kicked off my boots before pulling down my jeans. I rarely wore jocks, which I was grateful for at that moment.

I stood beside the bed and bent to grip the sheet so I could pull that fucker slowly down over my woman's body. I watched her shiver and her eyes heat for me as she bit her bottom lip.

With her hair spread out on the pillow, her stunning-as-fuck body on display, I could have come right then, but I wanted inside her first.

Christ, my dick jerked again at the thought of slipping in her without anything between us. Then my chest tightened when I thought of the possibility of her belly big and round with my child in her.

My kid.

I rubbed at my chest. I wanted that with her. The realisation almost knocked me to my knees. No other woman could have taken hold of my cold heart and warmed it, made me want things I never thought I would.

Shit, it wasn't the time, but soon. Fucking soon I'd plant my seed inside her.

Shaking off my thoughts, I leaned over my woman and took her mouth with mine. "This mine?" I asked against her lips.

"Yes," she answered.

Skimming my mouth down her neck, I bit and felt her shudder. I fuckin' loved bringing that reaction from her just from my mouth on her body.

Taking her nipple into my mouth, I asked, "This mine?" I glanced up as I sucked on it to see her nod. I pulled back and narrowed my gaze. "Want words, Tiny."

She licked her lips. "Yes, Dallas, it's yours."

I palmed her free breast and then glided my mouth down to her stomach. She sucked it in and quivered as I nibbled on her skin.

Lower still, while I kept rolling her breasts and pinching her nipples with one hand, I shifted my mouth to her mound and kissed it.

"This pussy mine?"

"Oh yeah," she said breathlessly.

"Nice and bare for me." Splaying my free hand over her mound, I then slid one finger straight into her tight, wet pussy. She arched and moaned. "Yeah, this pussy is mine. Means I can do what I want with it." She nodded. Smiling, I took my hand away only to slap it down on her mound, ripping a gasp from her and making sure my finger hit her clit. I rubbed my palm over it to take the sting away. If her eyes weren't hot with desire, I'd swear she'd laser me with her glare. "My pussy still?"

"Yes."

Another slap where I rubbed hard at her clit to bring more pleasure and take out the pain a little. She cried out at my touch. With her eyes closed, she wiggled on the bed, bringing her pussy up higher to me.

"Eyes," I ordered harshly. She opened them and met my gaze. As I let go of her tit, I brought my hand to my hard cock and jerked my palm up and down. Her heated eyes flicked to watch what I did. As a reward, I trailed my fingers to her opening and slipped two in deep, burying them as far as I could.

"Yes," she whispered.

"Gonna fuck your mouth while I finger fuck your pussy."

"Please," she begged like a good girl and licked her lips, her eyes still on my cock.

Shuffling up the bed, I knelt on the mattress, a hand to the side of her head. Since my woman was tied, which I loved, I gripped my dick and pressed it down to her lips. She sucked it in eagerly. She *wanted* to wet her man's cock with her mouth. Fucking perfect.

As I thrust into her mouth and pulled back, I slid my fingers inside of her with the same rhythm.

"Fuck," I bit out through clenched teeth. Feeling her mouth

around me was goddamn amazing. "Yeah, like that, fuckin' suck me."

I slammed my fingers deep inside her and arched them up. She hummed her moan around my dick and lifted her hips off the bed.

"Jesus," I hissed and ripped my cock from her mouth. I also slipped my fingers from her. I knew she was close to coming. I could feel her walls just start to clench. But I wanted to be inside her when she did. Quickly moving to between her legs, I slid right on in, balls deep, tearing a deep grunt from me and causing my woman to gasp.

"Love the feel of your pussy," I said before I sucked her skin just above her nipple into my mouth and bit down hard. "Love your body, darlin', but it needs my marks on it once again."

"Please," she begged, arching her back and offering up her other breast. "Need your marks, but need you to move more, my Viking man."

Slowly, I slid out of her, to just where the tip of my cock touched her entrance.

Looking down at my woman spread for me on the bed, I told her, "Never felt content in life, was always looking for something to make my life right. Just never knew what I needed was you."

"Dallas," she whispered, and then cried out when I thrust into her hard, over and over. "Oh god. Shit, I'm...." she moaned. Her eyes held mine as she came on my cock and in them I saw what she felt for me, and it fuckin' shone bright.

"Christ," I bit through clenched teeth and kept her gaze as my jizz squirted inside my woman. With one last slow thrust, I said, "You were mine right from the start."

She smiled. "And you were mine. Now untie me. Our bodies have a lot more reacquainting to do, and I need to touch you. Mark you as mine like you have on me."

My dick hardened, liking that thought a lot.

"How long you stayin'?" I asked, slipping my cock free and letting my woman loose.

"For a week. Do you know this is the first time, to outsiders, we actually meet and fall madly in love? So you better woo me and do it good. It'll explain why I'm suddenly dating a biker from Melbourne who will travel to Sydney often to visit, and why I'm willing to move to Melbourne for him."

I snorted. "I'll do fuckin' anything if it means I see you more."

She wrapped her arms around my shoulders and brought me down on top of her before I managed to untie her legs. "Glad you said anything because I have a favour to ask. Julian wants—"

Leaning in, I take her bottom lip between my teeth. "Do not push me too far, woman."

She grinned her cheeky grin and kissed me, deep, long, and just the way I liked it.

Hell, who'd have thought I'd be falling over myself to be with a woman? I was used to walking out on any situation that even hinted at a relationship, and now I was running right into one, straight into the arms of the woman who drove me crazy with worry, who pissed me off and teased me. However, I wouldn't have it any other fucking way.

She was it for me. She was mine.

SNEAK PEEK — HEAR ME OUT

HAWKS MC: CAROLINE SPRINGS CHARTER: BOOK 5

Prologue

BEAST

Rage and fear boiled up inside of me as I punched the door open. The room was full of people, but I couldn't find it in me to care who saw me losing my shit. It wasn't every fucking day when a person woke and couldn't hear shit, and I knew it wasn't just a blocked ear or some crap like that. It was serious. When my head had been spinning earlier, I'd thought a quick nap would make it better like all the other times. Then bam. Nothing but silence when I woke.

My heart thundered in my chest. I rubbed the back of my neck while stalking through the common room at the compound. I needed out. I had to get away to seek help.

Fuck. I was scared.

What if the doctor says I won't hear anymore?

Jesus. I couldn't even go there. I was out the door to the

SNEAK PEEK — HEAR ME OUT

compound and heading towards my ride when a hand landed on my shoulder causing me to jump like a damn pussy. I spun around to find Dallas, Dive, and Vicious in my personal space.

Christ.

Shit. Fuck me.

Their mouths moved, but I couldn't hear shit.

My gut churned. My heart beat so goddamn hard I laid a hand over my chest.

With wide eyes, I backed up a step. My eyes caught Mena coming up beside her man Dive. She grabbed his arm and said something to him. All men looked down at her, and Dive replied with something.

Fuck. I couldn't hear.

Clenching my jaw tightly, so I didn't cry like a little girl, I swiftly turned and bolted for my ride. If they were yelling for me, I didn't have a bloody clue nor did I care. I wanted answers. Needed them.

Riding towards the hospital, worry seeped into my veins, consuming me. If I couldn't hear, I'd be useless. I wouldn't be able to help out my brothers.

Fuck me.

Fuck.

My whole life I'd kept quiet for one main reason. I hadn't liked how I talked. But it was more than that. More than the sound and nothing to do with my accent. Things with my brain didn't connect right with my mouth, and sometimes I'd say shit but meant it as something else. It didn't bother me being silent. My brothers accepted it, but already I was wishing I had talked more.

Shit, even with all the teasing I got as a kid, I wished I'd talked more. Life could be bloody cruel. Not only could kids be ruthless, but so could adults. My dad didn't beat me, but he was a dick about the way I spoke. A dick day in and out when I'd stuff up what I wanted to say or stutter over shit when I tried to get it right. My mum was a gem, but my dad... fucking arsehole. Lost count of the times he'd smack me in the back of the head and yell, "Spit it out right!"

I shouldn't have let them get to me.

Christ, I should have talked more.

After finding a parking spot, I climbed off my ride and found a car pulling in beside me. My glare turned to it, and Mena clambered out of Dive's vehicle. Her lips moved, her eyes shone with panic, and her hands moved all over the place. I pulled my brows down and shook my head at her.

She stopped just in front of me. Her hands and fingers did some shit in front of her, but I didn't have a clue what, and then I saw her sigh. She lay a single palm on my arm. I didn't need her worry. Shrugging off her hold, I started towards the doors. Then a hand grabbed me with a force I didn't expect her to have. She pulled me around to face her, drew her hand up and tapped her mouth. I looked there. Slowly, she mouthed, "Let me help."

My heart did a double beat that hurt.

Did she know I couldn't hear?

Pulling my phone from my pocket, I looked up her number and realised I didn't have it. She slid my phone from my hand and pressed her fingers over it for a few moments before turning it to show me.

In a text, she wrote out: **You can't hear, can you?**

Slowly, I closed my eyes, pain slicing my chest. Opening them, I looked up at her and shook my head.

Her smile was sad as she nodded and typed something else into the phone. When she passed it back over, I read it. **Let's go in and find out why.**

Fucking hell.

She needed to leave. I was good at dealing with shit on my own. I didn't need a brother's old lady tagging along trying to fix me.

The phone was thrust back in front of my face. **I'm not leaving. Deal with it.**

I found myself snorting. Mena was finally growing into her biker babe status. She'd first been meek and mild. Since then, it seemed she was becoming stubborn as shit.

With a frustrated groan, one I couldn't hear myself, I nodded and started for the doors once again, with Mena matching my strides beside me.

MENA

Ever since Beast had come home from Sydney, after helping Dallas and Melissa, I had noticed there was something wrong. He'd acted the same, smiling when he was with his brothers, working out in the mechanical business when he had to, but staying his silent self. However, I'd also noticed times when dizziness would overcome him. He'd find something to hold on to until it passed. He wasn't a man a woman could get to know; he kept to himself a lot, except with his brothers, especially Knife, but even with that bond something had changed. Since they'd been back, I hardly saw them together. I wondered if something had happened between the two of them. Only what, I didn't know.

Kalen had seen me one day watching Beast. Stupidly, and kind of jokingly, he'd asked if I had a crush on Beast and if I did, he would beat the man black and blue. Of course I told him how ridiculous he was being. I also told him that I had a feeling something was going on with Beast. He'd smiled and said, "Sunshine, love you. But leave the brother alone."

I couldn't do as my man had asked though. Beast was dealing with things he didn't need to on his own, and I wanted to help him.

When Beast had stormed from the bedroom area at the compound earlier, I knew, knew something bad had happened. And as I watched his fast pace through the room, he took no notice of his brothers, nor some of the women calling him. Then it was as if something clicked; I got up and raced after him. When I found him and his brothers outside, I saw Beast's puzzled expression as his brothers tried to talk to him.

When I had been working in childcare, there had been a little girl who had been deaf. She was timid but sweet, so I'd made an effort to learn sign language so I could talk with her.

Why she popped into my mind as I watched Beast leave didn't register immediately, not until I saw her expressions of confusion and frustration mirrored on Beast's face.

I realised then, as he stormed off from his brothers, that he couldn't hear a single word said.

Grabbing Kalen's arm, I whispered in a rushed voice, "Let me follow him. He doesn't need a brother right now."

"I don't think—"

"Please, Kalen. Please trust me in this."

He searched my face and finally nodded. Knowing his keys had been in his pocket, I grabbed them quickly and ran for his car. I was surprised I'd made it to the hospital car park just after Beast. At first, I thought he would have told me to get lost, even when I demanded to go in with him. So I was shocked when he nodded. Then again, the fear in his eyes was palpable.

While we waited, I sat beside Beast as he bounced his leg up and down, biting his thumbnail again and again while his eyes flicked wildly around the room.

Knowing him... actually, knowing he was a Hawks member, there was no doubt he was searching for potential threats. Despite my need to reassure him that nothing could harm us in there, I didn't, thinking at least his search kept his mind occupied.

"Maddox Lawson?"

Since I'd seen the paperwork Beast had filled out, I knew that was his name. Glancing at him, I saw he had his eyes over at the front door. Reaching out, I tapped his arm. He spun his gaze to me, and I gestured to the doctor. We both walked into the emergency room.

"Hi, I'm Doctor Spencer." The doctor smiled as we entered, his hand flying out to the bed. He eyed Beast in his biker gear as Beast sat on the bed. I stood behind it while the doctor sat in the swivel chair opposite the bed. "What seems to be the problem?"

Beast's brows dipped low, so I shifted forward and said, "Be— Maddox is having trouble hearing."

"Hmm." The doctor flipped open whatever file he had for Beast. "Says here he was in an accident nearly five weeks ago and had a bad head injury." He looked up. "Has there been any other problems?"

"I've seen him get dizzy a few times," I offered.

I jumped when Beast slapped a hand to the bed. Blushing, since we were talking about him like he wasn't there, I typed into his phone: **Sorry. The doctor said you were in an accident and asked if anything else was going on. I told him I've noticed that you've been getting dizzy.** I quickly handed it to him.

After he had read it, he nodded and then deleted what I had and wrote back.

Taking the phone, I read it out to the doctor: **Headaches.** I looked up, concerned.

Doctor Spencer nodded and wrote a few things down before

he suddenly stood and said, "I just have to speak with another doctor, and we'll need to run some tests. I'll be back."

I typed into the phone what the doctor said and handed it to Beast. He read it, dropped the phone to the bed, and then ran a hand over his face.

Without thinking, I signed that everything would be okay. His eyes narrowed on my hands. Biting my bottom lip, I cringed and picked up the phone again. **Sorry, I was using sign language. You don't know it?**

After he had read it, he shook his head, but then typed something back. I read it as he did. **I never needed it. I could hear and talk.**

My eyes widened. I grabbed the phone. **You can talk?**

Pain darkened his eyes, he nodded. "I talk don't right." His face screwed up in frustration. He couldn't hear himself, yet he knew he'd said it wrong. He snapped the phone from me and typed out: **I don't talk right. My words get mixed up. I know what I want to say, but it comes out wrong.**

I typed: **Is it all the time?**

He shook his head, clenching his jaw. I could tell he didn't like talking about it, so even though I wanted to ask a million questions, I didn't. He had enough to worry about.

With the phone in my hand, I thought about what I wanted to say. He needed to know that everyone around him who was important wouldn't care how he spoke. If his hearing loss was forever, he should feel comfortable to still speak.

Standing from the chair, I paced the room and typed into the phone. **No matter the outcome today, you have people who will support you. Even if you don't feel you could talk to them (though, I think they wouldn't care how you spoke), there are other ways to communicate. Like sign language. These are just thoughts for now. We don't know anything yet. But I want you to know, we all care.**

A nurse came through the curtain. She smiled at me, and when she spotted Beast, the big, brooding man on the bed, her eyes widened.

"Um." She started and then licked her lips as her gaze travelled over him. "I came to take your blood." When I glanced to Beast, I saw he sat glaring at her.

Smiling, I nodded to the nurse and added, "It's fine." While she went about it, I handed the phone back to Beast.

His jaw clenched a few times, and after he had finished reading, he placed the phone on the bed. When he pulled his head up to meet my gaze with his own, I saw moisture in them. My heart clenched for the large man. As soon as the nurse moved away, I was at his side in seconds, and without a thought, I wrapped my arms around his waist. It took a few beats until I felt his arms wind around my shoulders.

BEAST

Heart of gold. My brother was fucking lucky to have a woman like Mena. Christ, to have her there with me meant a lot, and I wasn't sure I could ever repay her. However, I wasn't certain I could let her words in. My brothers may not care how I spoke, but I did. I sounded like a dick. She tried to give me hope to hold on to, but I knew I was fucked.

Never would I hear again.

Fucking hell.

It hurt. Christ, did it hurt.

When the doctors came back in hours later, and after a heap more tests, some from different doctors, I had Mena write down everything they said, with me watching over her shoulder. I wasn't surprised when she wrote I wouldn't hear again. It'd been due to the bike accident I'd had before I went to Sydney. Due to the head injury, they called it a sensorineural hearing loss. As they handed Mena some pamphlet shit about it all, I sat there with no thought running through my mind.

I was finally numb.

ACKNOWLEDGEMENTS

To Becky Johnson and her amazing team at Hot Tree Editing, thank you for all you do!

Lindsey Lawson, I always appreciate your help involved in each and every book.

To my Lila Muffkateers group, thank you for all your support with Hawks.

ALSO BY LILA ROSE

Hawks MC: Ballarat Charter
Holding Out (FREE) Zara and Talon
Climbing Out: Griz and Deanna
Finding Out (novella) Killer and Ivy
Black Out: Blue and Clarinda
No Way Out: Stoke and Malinda
Coming Out (novella) Mattie and Julia

Hawks MC: Caroline Springs Charter
The Secret's Out: Pick, Billy and Josie
Hiding Out: Dodge and Willow
Down and Out: Dive and Mena
Living Without: Vicious and Nary
Walkout (novella) Dallas and Melissa
Hear Me Out: Beast and Knife
Breakout (novella) Handle and Della
Fallout: Fang and Poppy

Standalones related to the Hawks MC
Out of the Blue (Lan, Easton, and Parker's story)
Out Gamed (novella) (Nancy and Gamer's story)
Outplayed (novella) (Violet and Travis's story)

Romantic comedies
Making Changes

Making Sense

Fumbled Love

Trinity Love Series
Left to Chance
Love of Liberty (novella)

Paranormal
Death (with Justine Littleton)
In The Dark

CONNECT WITH LILA ROSE

Webpage: www.lilarosebooks.com

Facebook: http://bit.ly/2du0taO

Instagram: www.instagram.com/lilarose78/

Goodreads:

www.goodreads.com/author/show/7236200.Lila_Rose